DEATH SONG

Matt Case, a Cree half-breed, journeyed a long way to visit his father's homeland. But the Gila Plain wasn't what he expected, nor was the brutal, cheating way of Grod Mitcham, the ramrod of the Coomer Spills ranch. When Matt reached the town of White Basin, he witnessed a cruel killing which affected the creed of his mixed blood. He knew he could turn his back or get involved and face the inevitable bloody showdown. The decision he was forced to make would bend the will of even this man of steel.

ABE DANCER

DEATH SONG

Complete and Unabridged

LINFORD
Leicester

First published in Great Britain in 2003 by
Robert Hale Limited
London

First Linford Edition
published 2005
by arrangement with
Robert Hale Limited
London

British Library CIP Data

Dancer, Abe
    Death song.—Large print ed.—
    Linford western library
    1. Western stories
    2. Large type books
    I. Title
    823.9′2 [F]

ISBN 1–84395–618–7

Published by
F. A. Thorpe (Publishing)
Anstey, Leicestershire

Set by Words & Graphics Ltd.
Anstey, Leicestershire
Printed and bound in Great Britain by
T. J. International Ltd., Padstow, Cornwall

This book is printed on acid-free paper

1

Arizona

White Basin was located in the unforgiving Gila Plain territory. It lay low, circled by hills that trapped heat and dust in the south-west corner of Arizona. Tall agaves and mescal filtered the breezes that would have otherwise brought relief to the bleak settlement. The town had been located near the lower slopes of Eagle Tail Mountains, a few miles away from the dense timber-stands of pine and spruce from which a few townsfolk gleaned a living. In Matt Case's mind's eye, it was almost exactly as his father had described it to him many years ago, and in bewildering contrast to most of the country he'd ridden through in the five months since leaving Saskatchewan.

Matt's horse shifted under him but

he checked it, holding it quiet while he spared a thought for his father.

It was twenty-five years since Barker Case had heard tell of the fortunes being made up around the Great Lakes. From White Basin, he'd travelled the 1,500 miles north to Moose Jaw. There he traded his cow pony for a canoe and traps, paddled the Qu'Appelle to Flat Stone. That was near to where he'd meet Blue Sky, the Cree chieftain's daughter he'd later marry, who was to become Matt's mother.

Matt leaned forward and patted the neck of his horse, recalled the dying words of his father. They were cheerless words, which had stayed with him for many years.

'The big company's . . . bosslopers are movin' in, son. They're spread out all along the Red River . . . along the border. There's no room for the free trappers any more. You ain't got your ma, so just go,' the old man had said. 'If you ever make it to White Basin, don't take much heed. Look to the country about. Look in any direction. Make it *your* country.'

So now Matt Case *had* got here. Fully grown, and years later than he should have. Perhaps *too* late to make any part of it his own country. The horse shifted again, impatient to get moving, wearied by the heat and another day's ride. It wanted water and feed, so Matt gave it its head down the slope, on to the rutted trail that led to White Basin.

Horse and rider flickered in the heat shimmer off the land. The horse was an iron-grey mare, well-built and despite its weariness was sure of foot. Matt was tall and slim, rode at ease in the saddle. He had the sun-burned skin of a mixed-blood and his dark, deep-set eyes looked around with the confidence of a man who'd seen much. He wore a mail-order black suit because that's what you wore when you travelled beyond Flat Stone, he'd decided.

Two miles out from White Basin, Matt let his horse pick a solitary trail

3

across the plain. When he eventually rode into the town, he kept to the west side of the main street, where there was shade from the slanting sun. The grey nickered, crow-hopped excitedly on getting near a street trough and Matt let it go for the water.

Two townsmen walked across the street towards him and Matt nodded civilly.

'Where can I get my horse took care of?' he asked.

'Lome's. Turn left past Scully's Rooms . . . that's where *you* drink. There ain't no choice,' one of the men said bluntly.

Matt said thanks, unsure of who 'no choice' applied to. He drew his horse from the tepid water and walked on, clasped one hand to the horn of his saddle. With his hat brim bent low, he looked along the main street. He glanced coolly at the paint-peeled store-fronts and bleached boardwalks, the overall dried-out decay. He passed Scully's Rooms and considered taking a drink. But he thought of his horse first. He had little idea of how long he'd be staying in White Basin or what it had to offer, thought maybe he'd go back to the saloon a little later.

On the side of a building, an arrow pointed down a side-street. Under it was a sign that read: BULL LOME'S LIVERY STABLE.

Matt turned into the rank, muck-covered lane. With his usual caution, he pressed the palm of his left hand into the butt of his gun. It was a .45 Colt, which he had tucked snug in the glass-beaded blanket band he wore tied around his waist.

The town was quiet in this near-to-noon hour, with only a small number of people on the move. But when Matt was in sight of the open doors of the livery stable, someone suddenly staggered in front of him. From one side of the street, a man wavered then stopped, lurched forward, fell to his knees.

Matt saw he was an elder, a man with enough years to mean something to a mixed-blood Cree. And this old man was cowering, his pale watery eyes burning with fear. Then a gun fired, roared twice in the narrowness of the street. The bullets buried themselves in the ground either side of the old man's knees, kept him from moving.

Matt pulled on his horse's mane, made some comforting sounds. He twisted slightly in the saddle and, from his right and just behind him, four men appeared from a pole-fronted stable yard. One of them stepped forward challengingly and two others were holding back. The fourth was trying to quieten a bad-tempered chestnut gelding.

The first man took a brief, careless look at Matt. He was a big man who hesitated just for a moment, before waving Matt away. Then he pulled back his fist and piled his knuckles down hard into the back of the old man's neck.

The oldster didn't make a sound, just went down with his face driven hard into the dung-encrusted ground. But then he did cry out, as the big man kicked him in the legs, ribs, the side of his head. The two men who'd been standing back were watching Matt, were worried that he didn't like what was happening.

But it wasn't Matt's affair, and it was hardly his town. So he suggested dully:

'Why don't you leave the old feller alone? Looks to me like he's had enough.'

The man waited for Matt's words to sink in, then he turned on his heel. He bunched his fist and blew on his knuckles.

'Back off,' he said, boorishly.

Matt spared a quick look at the other two, saw the uncertainty in their faces. Then the big man reached down and pulled the old-timer from the dust. He held him with one hand, slapped his face with the other.

Matt leaned back, touched his horse's belly with his bootheels, lunged the animal forward. He swung the hard grey head to the left and the horse's shoulder smashed the tall man away. Matt swung from the saddle, stepped to one side, then forward quickly.

His right hand went out and cupped the man's throat, his left pistoned low into his midriff. The blow exploded the man's breath away, staggered him a step or two backwards. Matt turned quickly to see the expected advance of the other two men.

His left hand moved quickly to his waistband, drew his Colt. The two men stopped in their tracks. One of them was eyeing the big man behind Matt. Matt turned back to see that the man had pulled his own gun half-way from its holster.

'That'd be real stupid. Me with my gun already pointed at your gut an' all,' Matt pointed out.

The old man, who'd got to his feet, stood wheezing and watching, took a step back to lean against a building. Then he pushed himself straight away from the wall, and drew his own gun.

He chewed on some air as he tottered around. His eyes were rheumy, but hate-filled when he pulled the trigger. His bony wrist bucked and the bullet whistled high above and between the two other men. They cursed in unison, stared hard at Matt. But then the man who'd been holding the fractious gelding dropped its headstall, drew a pistol from his belt and fired in one violent movement.

The old man dropped his gun and clutched his knotty fingers at his shirt front. He let out a whisper of air, twisted futilely at his darkening shirt front.

He seemed to sniff at the air, then Matt thought he smiled. But he wasn't. He was saying something, grimacing as pain coursed through his gaunt frame. He was dying, crumpling to the ground, when Matt's shot ripped the horseminder's arm apart, sent the gelding rearing and bucking away down the side-street.

'I never done them no harm . . . never

. . . never stole cattle,' the old man had croaked. Then his dry lips ceased to move against the hard-packed dirt. His legs flinched once, then he died.

Matt grabbed the big man roughly, hurled him at his two companions. He raised his Colt, set the action.

The big man was rasping loudly. 'In hell's name, mister, I don't know who you are, but you just bought into a load o' somethin' bad.'

'I guess I did.' Matt told him. He looked past the men as someone turned into the side-street. This man was different, though. He carried a shotgun, wore a star on the lapel of his short plaid coat.

2

Dead End

Sheriff Emple walked fast, took notice of the stricken old man. He stopped just short of Matt, eyed him with professional assessment, then spoke to the big man.

'I might o' known. Speak to me, an' make it good,' he commanded.

The big man glared furiously at the lawman for a moment before he answered.

'This weren't my play, Sheriff. We came in here after a damned cattle-thief, an' we caught us one. It was Homer Welles.'

Emple looked sidelong at the pathetic form of Homer Welles. He spat sourly and cursed.

The big man was Grod Mitcham, and he carried on talking.

'So make sure you aim your spittin' an' cursin' right.' He pointed at Matt. 'It was him an' Welles. They stole some o' Coomer Spills's cattle . . . hid 'em up on Welles's ground. We followed their tracks into town. There'll be enough of them Phoenix buyers here. Them that ain't too watchful about the brands they're buyin'. You know that, Sheriff.'

Emple looked disappointed at Matt. 'Well?' he asked.

'I don't know what they're talkin' about,' Matt told him coolly. 'I do know the big plug-ugly here's a liar. As for the aged one . . . well, I've never seen him before. But that goes for all of 'em, an' that's the truth.'

'How'd you get involved?' the sheriff asked just as coolly.

'I just rode in . . . was followin' the livery stable sign. They came out . . . started bulldoggin' the old feller. He drew his gun all right, but he was beat so bad he couldn't see proper. They weren't good odds, Sheriff. Don't matter what the old 'un did. The dink there with half an arm's a killer.'

Emple turned his attention to the man Matt indicated with his gun.

'What you got to say, Chawke? Is what he says right?' he growled.

Chawke was holding his shattered arm tight against his chest. Pain distorted his face, drained him of colour.

'I need me a doctor,' he groaned. 'Grod told it right. They must o' been stealin' Spills's cattle. Welles went for his gun, and I had to shoot. I didn't know I'd kill him, an' nobody's goin' to say any different. Now someone get me to Pease.'

'You heard him. Now get the *mestizo* in your jail, Sheriff,' Mitcham said, still breathing hard. 'An' you keep him there 'til Mr Spills come to take a look at him. Them tracks tell their own tale.'

Emple frowned, threw a worried look in Matt's direction as he answered sharply:

'You keep your big mouth to yourself, Grod, else I'll walk away, leave

13

you to sort it out amongst yourselves. You really want that?' he asked with a shrewd edge to his voice.

The sheriff was right in his caution. Matt didn't like Mitcham's reference to his mixed blood. His eyes turned black, bored through the big man.

But for the moment Mitcham had the protection of a county sheriff.

'You know how Mr Spills deals with cattle-thieves, Shave?' he said. 'If there ain't a cottonwood handy, he'll drag 'em 'til their skin turns red.' With that, he looked hard at Matt, licked his lips at his dark humour.

Matt pushed his Colt back into his waistband. Emple saw the look that told him that Grod Mitcham was a dead man if he didn't step in. It was so obvious the stranger didn't want to use his gun, had got some other bad way of killing.

Almost reluctantly Emple swung his shotgun at Matt.

'I know what you're thinkin', stranger. But I'll take that Colt anyways. Hand it over,' he said firmly.

'What about *one arm*?' Matt asked, even and slow.

'There ain't no doubt it was old Homer drew a gun first. There's enough witnesses for that. Much as I'd like, I ain't holdin' Chawke for anythin'. Anyways, leave him standin' much longer, an' he'll bleed to death.'

'I told you, Sheriff, I just rode in. I was lookin' to get oats for the grey.'

The sheriff looked as though he was getting bored.

'Yeah, that's as maybe,' he said. 'But there's this other matter o' the stolen Spills beef. I can't just turn you loose an' you know it.' Emple drew back the twin hammers of his shotgun. 'Now, last time, gimme your gun.'

Matt made some barely audible sounds, then a short intake of breath as he decided. He took a few steps towards the sheriff.

'You take it,' he said. 'I don't give it to no one. There's a difference.'

'Yeah, I just bet there is,' Emple said

as he lifted the Colt, admired the glass-beaded waist band. 'What tribe's that?' he asked considerately.

'Cree,' Matt told him. 'My ma,' he added, knowing the sheriff was wondering.

'The Red River eh? Well, that's a hell of a long ways off, son. I ain't ever been further north than Wolf Hole, myself,' Emple said, with a half-smile.

The moment Emple had Matt's gun, Mitcham grimaced sourly and his mouth started working again.

'Now we'll see how many tongues *you* got,' he smirked. 'See how you holler when a loop o' hemp starts squeezin' your neck.'

'Get out o' my way,' the sheriff snapped. 'Any o' you men make a move I don't like, an' I'll blast your goddamn hides. This is a lawful take now, an' I'm handlin' it. You'll do best to get your stories off pat, 'cause I'm warnin' you now. If there's any lyin' been done, you'll find little comfort in this town from now on.'

Mitcham held up his hand in mock entreaty. 'We got 'em all but branded, Sheriff. You see if we ain't.'

Emple nudged Matt in the side, motioned for him to move on.

Matt held out his hand, waited for the grey to come back to him. He led it back to the main street, muttering about having to wait for a rub down and feed, that he'd take care of it. As he turned on to the dry, grey boardwalk, he turned to see Emple point his shotgun to the right. He headed for the jailhouse, ignored the interested small crowd who'd gathered. They watched him in curious dumb silence, but one of them stepped forward and spat at his feet. He stopped, but another nudge from Emple made him go on.

He carefully hitched his horse outside the jailhouse while staring back down the street. Then he pushed aside the already half-open door, walked into the small, heat-choked building, didn't understand why Emple had called it the 'cooler'.

Emple turned the key in the first of three cells. He took off his sweat-stained hat, cursed and wiped his gleaming forehead. Standing at his desk, he flicked and fumbled at some papers.

'Right here ain't the best spot in town, mister. So you can start by tellin' me what I don't already know. What's your name?'

'Matt. Matt Case.' Matt didn't think a Cree name would help him much in the circumstances — wasn't the time to go *Injun*.

'How come you met up with Homer Welles?'

'I already told you, Sheriff. The one called Mitcham was givin' him a real beatin'. I suggested that he leave him alone. Said I thought he'd taken enough.'

'Seems a fair request. What happened then?'

'All four of 'em started to act real hostile-like. I think they wanted to kill that helpless old feller all on their own.

What was his name . . . Homer?'

'Yeah. Homer Welles.' Emple looked hard at Matt. 'An' you never seen him before? You're stickin' to that story?'

'I'm just stickin' to the truth, Sheriff. I'm hopin' you're goin' to do the same. I ain't takin' any of your Choctaw justice for somethin' I ain't done.'

'It'll be the *truth* that gets its chance, mister,' the sheriff said with a wry smile. 'But I'm tellin' you, against the statements o' those four, you need a better excuse than takin' your mount for a feed.'

Matt looked around him, through the bars at the bleak, featureless surroundings. He remembered his pa telling him not to take much heed of the surroundings. 'I never did make the stable. Can you take care o' my horse?' he asked.

Emple nodded. 'Yeah. I'll get it done. Now, you just rode in, Matt Case, so maybe you can tell me where you been the last few days . . . up 'til this mornin?'

Matt's shoulders heaved at the setback. For the last two weeks he'd ridden from Lake Powell and the Utah border, made lone camps. He'd seen a cattle drive trailing south along the Colorado River towards Yuma, but he'd spoken to no one since leaving Salt Lake City.

When he didn't give an immediate answer, Emple set out more circumstances.

'Well, it don't improve matters. That outfit you just crossed? They're Spills men, an' Coomer ain't exactly what you'd call a feeder steer, if you get my meanin'. When Grod Mitcham tells him what happened here, he'll come down like a blue norther.'

Matt immediately wanted to ask where the sheriff would be during all this but, deciding he was in deep enough, held his tongue again. He stretched out on the dust-packed crib, realized he was badly placed. If the rancher called Coomer Spills was that powerful, how would Shave Emple stack up against him, what back-up did he have? Whatever, Matt didn't intend to be hanged, that was for sure. He was a fast learner, and, not for many years, had he let other men cheat or beat him.

Emple reached for his shotgun beside his desk, placed it on top of the papers. Then he pulled his revolver and checked the cylinder, thoughfully pushed it back down into his holster. He opened the jailhouse's sand-blasted window, blinked at a zephyr of hot dust.

Ten minutes later, two men delivered Homer Welles's body to the jailhouse. Emple gave dubious thanks, asked them to take Matt's grey to the stable, get it looked after.

With a great deal of cursing and puffing, the sheriff laid out the dead old man in the cell next to Matt.

'Old goat,' he muttered. 'About as likely a cattlethief as Tad Lincoln.'

Matt watched the sheriff from under the brim of his hat, said nothing. He was truly in two minds about old men dying or getting themselves killed. The white man in him doubted there was a greater place to go to, thought it just moved you further along the mortal line.

He pulled his hat over his face, clasped his fingers behind his head, and closed his eyes. In the small, dark world he recalled the time when he'd first realized his own father was getting old.

Barker Case had taken him to the burial ground of Blue Sky. It was an eerie, silent place, and the remains of Matt's mother were laid on a platform of logs in a black-branched tree. A blanket hung in tatters from the crumbling platform, touched a beaded band that had fallen to the ground beside the bones of a sacrificed pony. Matt had watched intrigued, as his pa kneeled to remove a fragment from the scattered pile.

At the time, there was so much Matt had wanted to ask about medicine and spiritual meanings, but he was embarrassed and unsure, because he was a child. That was when he'd noticed the wolfy greyness of his pa's hair, the deeply etched lines of his ageing.

The piece of bone had been made into the handle of a small clasp-knife that Matt still kept deep in his pocket. Now, lying in his close darkness, he envisioned a cunning smirk across Grod Mitcham's face, and shuddered. He shook himself from his day-dream, pulled his hat away from his face. For a moment he reflected on allowing himself to be drawn into trouble. He'd only been in White Basin an hour or so, but he swore that before he left, he'd have a go at shifting that look off Mitcham's face.

3

Medicine Man

Except childbirth, tooth-pulling and sickly calves, Harold Pease MD didn't regard anything less than amputations as too serious. 'I can take it off now. But if it's fixin' you're after, come back when I'm less busy' was a quoted truism from his sawbone days in the Civil War.

He pushed up out of his chair, got flustered when the cowhand, Reefer Chawke piled into his private room back of his surgery. Through the door, he could see Grod Mitcham waiting on the back porch with Niles Stockman and Clem Rollo.

Chawke turned his bloodied arm towards him.

'I been hit. This goddamn arm's fallin' apart. See to it, Doc,' he growled.

Pease had a brief look at the man's shattered limb. 'Looks like someone already done just that,' he said, as calm as he could.

'Just do it!' Chawke yelled. 'Stop the pain an' the bleedin'.'

'We'll use the surgery,' the doc said. He walked into the annexed room, rinsed his hands under the faucet. Then he slowly reached for a towel.

Chawke followed him, stood close by, cursing under his breath. He was blanching with pain, his face greasy-cold with sweat. He was also grinding his teeth at Pease's casual disregard for the torture he was enduring.

'Goddamn you, Pease. You waitin' for the sepsis?'

'That's what it'll be if I don't clean my hands,' Pease said calmly. 'There's plenty come worse off than you, today. You the one who killed Homer?' he then asked more sharply.

'You know about that?'

'I knew he'd been shot dead . . . not who pulled the trigger.'

Chawke was taking short, sharp breaths. He glared at the doctor. 'He drew on me. I just defended myself.'

With that Pease took hold of the cuff of Chawke's shirt. He lifted it up, tried for a closer look at the bullet wound between the man's wrist and elbow. Chawke let out a gasp of pain and took a step backwards.

'What the hell you doin', you idiot. The goddamn arm's broke . . . been smashed with a bullet, anyone can see that. Give me somethin' for the pain, before you start meddlin'.'

'Well, you best remember, sonny, it's *this* meddlin' idiot who's the only one around here can do somethin' about your discomfort.' The doc smiled cruelly. 'Anyways, a top ranny who's tough enough to take out Homer Welles in a gunfight, can endure a twinge or two.' Before Chawke could respond, Pease went on sharply: 'But if you want that help, it'll cost you ten dollars.'

'Ten dollars?'

'Yep. The bones're busted, needs

some fancy work. It's ten dollars, an' I hope you're carryin' it in your *left* pocket. Take it or leave it, mister, it ain't my body.'

Chawke gasped. 'Why, you blood-sucker,' he ranted, 'I'll . . . ' But the man stopped short of his threat when Grod Mitcham strode into the surgery.

'I can hear you squealin' on the street,' Mitcham said tetchily.

'He wants ten dollars for fixin' my arm,' Chawke rasped. 'He ain't a doctor, he's an old army cut-throat.'

'An' I want it before I start,' Pease said coolly, his manner matching Mitcham's.

Mitcham drew in a sharp breath and turned on Chawke.

'Just wash the wound. Do it yourself,' he said, rushing out his words. 'We'll just take some painkillin' stuff. Waste o' time comin' to this dude set-up. We should o' gone to the livery for a saddle-stitch. He'd o' charged five dollars for a tight, lastin' job.'

Pease almost smiled. If only he knew,

he thought. 'I just told him. It looks like there's bad lesion trouble . . . all sorts o' trauma, beside broken bone,' he said instead.

Mitcham made a grab at the lapels of Pease's coat. He shoved him into a high-backed chair with casters which slewed noisily up against a side wall.

'Not satisfied with Homer Welles?' Pease asked, the contempt evident in his voice.

Mitcham stepped forward, sharply struck one of the doctor's shins with the toe of his boot.

'You shut your mouth. Find somethin' to disinfect his wound. An' do it now,' he said.

Mitcham went to a glass-fronted cabinet and looked at the labels on bottles. He opened the door and pulled out a bottle of laudanum, showed it to Pease.

'Forget it, we'll take this. Let's go, Reefer,' he said, and tossed a silver dollar on to Pease's desk. 'Think yourself lucky,' he said without explanation.

Pease glared defiantly. 'A bully's

always a coward, Mitcham,' he told him. 'I've seen 'em all in my time. An' there's one thing they all got in common. They die many times, an' you ain't no different. Your time's comin'. It's just a question of how far away.'

Mitcham's jaw tightened and he hesitated a moment. Then he went, shoving Chawke ahead of him. He clumped down the steps of Pease's property, shouted at Clem Rollo.

'Get back to Mr Spills. Tell him what's happened. Tell him we'll sort out the drifter. We'll bring the supply wagon in early tomorrow. And have the boys make a gather on the cattle . . . tell him what we found.'

Rollo went off at a canter, and Mitcham led Chawke and Niles Stockman down the street to Scully's Rooms.

'We'll wait here an hour,' he said. 'Then Niles, you go and bail out the *metis*.'

Stockman grimaced, repeated Mitcham's instruction. 'Bail out the *metis*?

I don't understand. Why we bailin' *him* out?'

'Because he's no good to us in Emple's jail.' Mitcham beckoned the bartender, ordered some beers. 'You'll get your chance Nils,' he continued. 'We'll bust him up some, when he gets out. Then we'll get him back on that grey o' his.' Mitcham could see both Stockman and Chawke eyeing him intently, still not completely understanding. 'We ain't got Welles any more, remember. So we need someone else. The *metis*'ll do fine.'

Stockman's mouth opened as he grasped Mitcham's plan. 'We got ourselves a pigeon to take the blame. We pull the big job, and he's there, prime an' sassy,' he said, grinning broadly.

Two beers were placed on the bar in front of the three men who stood indifferent to the stares of the other customers. Not one of them doubted that the ill feeling in White Basin was already running high against them. But when you worked for the Spills outfit, it went with the territory. It started from the time Coomer Spills cut himself off from the range and the town, became his own law.

'You drink some o' this,' Mitcham said, pulling out the bottle of laudanum that he'd taken from Doc Pease's surgery. 'When we get you back to the ranch, we'll get that arm seen to proper,' he told Chawke with little obvious feeling.

* * *

Doc Pease limped across the hot sandy street. His face was screwed up, tilted away from the low glare of the sun. His leg hurt from where Mitcham had kicked him. Homer Welles had been a friend of his, and Pease knew it was ludicrous for anyone to believe he'd been involved in something to get shot for.

He stepped through the open door of the jailhouse to find Shave Emple seated behind his desk. The sheriff, with an unlit corn-cob pipe in the corner of his mouth, raised his eyes wearily. He held a dipping pen, had been concentrating on writing up a ledger.

He nodded at Pease and a deep crease furrowed his brow.

'You took your time,' he grumbled. 'But before you say anythin', Harry, there was nothin' I could do about Chawke killin' old Homer. It had been done when I got there.'

'Yeah, well I guess our legs just ain't got the full, fast movement in 'em any more. Shave,' Pease answered sardonically. He looked through to the cells, had another look at Matt. Having his practice at the north end of town, he'd seen Matt ride in. He'd been interested because, for one reason or another, lone riders were rare in that part of the country. He'd taken note of the man's appearance, his engaged bearing. Here was a stranger who'd travelled a long way. And to get to White Basin was an added curiosity.

'You ain't no cattle-rustler are you, son?' he asked Matt directly.

Matt was lying very still on the cot. Only his eyes moved, took in the doc as he spoke.

'No, I ain't. Sheriff thinks otherwise though, an' that's what counts from in here.'

'Ha.' Pease laughed. 'Even *I* know, all Indians are horse-thieves.' Then he turned to confront the sheriff.

But Emple got in first. 'I can do without your droll opinions . . . your intervention, if you're thinkin' on it, Harry,' he said.

'You're a damn fool, Shave, an' most o' this town knows it. A good sheriff yep, but a damn fool, nonetheless. You really believe what them Spills hands got to say . . . Grod Mitcham in particular? They all treat this town as if it's their own private robbers' roost. They're goddamn irritants at best. Never been far away from a killin' at worst, an' that's now.'

Emple bit hard on the stem of his

33

pipe. His face coloured as he leaned across the desk, banged the frame of Matt's .45 down on to the already deeply dented desk-top.

'Listen, what I had to do — ' he began.

'Close your chops, Shave. You listen to me for a bit,' Pease cut in. 'I was out front havin' myself a smoke, when I saw old Homer ride into town. He came in past the chandler's . . . other end o' town. That's what he would o' done if he'd been comin' from his ranch. But I saw this stranger too, an' there was a good half-hour between 'em. He comes in from the north though, where *he* would o' done if he'd come off the Colorado trail.'

The sheriff sat quietly contemplating his desk top, rubbing his chin, inspecting the bowl of his pipe.

'Come on, Shave.' Pease persisted. 'You already heard him say he ain't no rustler. I believe him, why can't you? In fact, why don't you release him, let him get about his business? The only harm he's likely to do now, will be to Spills's crew.'

Matt stirred himself, rolled from his cot. He took a step up to the bars of his cell, looked intensely at Doc Pease for a moment. 'I'm obliged to you,' he said.

Pease held out his hand. 'Name's Harry Pease. For my sins, town MD.' he said.

Matt pushed his own fist through the bars to shake hands. 'I'm Matt Case. Just tell me why,' he said simply.

'Always prided myself on havin' the measure of a man,' Pease answered him. 'Sheriff knows it too. He also knows I don't condone wastin' town's money. That's what'll happen if there's a court case over this.'

Emple moved out from behind his desk, dabbed at the sweaty sheen across his face.

'Mitcham said he followed *two* sets of tracks into town from Homer's place. He said Case here was in league with him.'

'Grod Mitcham's a liar . . . about as honest as Injun whiskey, an' we all know it.' Pease turned casually to Matt. 'Sorry, son, no offence meant,' he offered.

'None taken,' Matt accepted.

'If you want . . . if it'll help, I'll document those facts,' Pease told Emple. 'Whichever way it breaks, young Matt here don't deserve to be locked up for goin' to old Homer's aid. If it was you or me, Shave, we'd o' done the same thing. We'd be dead cause of it, but that's the only difference.'

Emple took his hands away from Matt's gun, gripped the edges of his desk, He was undecided as to what action to take and Pease knew it. Pease, aware of the lawman's dilemma, stepped past him and pulled a ring of keys from a wall peg.

But Emple pushed himself up and away from his desk. He reached out a big hand, clasped it around Pease's wrist.

'Goddamnit Doc. I'm sittin' here willin' to listen, not for you to take over the jail . . . not by a long spit.'

Pease sighed wearily, dropped the keys on to the end of the desk.

'Mulehead Emple. What else is there for you to listen to? We said it all.'

'There's plenty to be said, Doc. I got to put this side o' things to Mitcham. Then, dependin' on what he says . . . what we work out, I'll either release Case or keep him here for trial.' Emple smiled patiently at Pease. 'As a doctor, Harry, you'd make a half-decent bull-dogger. Now leave me alone to get on with my business.'

Pease grimaced exasperatedly as Emple hung the keys back on the wall hook.

'I ain't finished just yet,' he said, winked friendly-like at Matt. 'Tell *me* what happened, son. I suddenly got myself a bedside manner.'

I'll go lie down again then,' Matt said wryly.

4

Torture Trail

'I saw Welles bein' crowded . . . figured there was too many for him,' Matt explained to Doc Pease. 'I told Mitcham that, but he weren't impressed. I had to step in . . . stop the beatin'. The old man made a break for it, although he could only just about stand. An' that's the curious thing about it.'

'What's so curious about what?' Pease asked.

'Well, he could . . . should o' got clear, but he didn't. He stopped an' pulled a gun, he was so stirred up. I could see it in his eyes. He managed to get off a shot too. That's when Chawke killed him.'

'Homer said somethin' did he . . . before he died?' Pease asked.

'He didn't have the time to say

much. He mumbled somethin' though . . . as he fell . . . somethin' about him not being a cattle-stealer.' Matt turned his head towards Pease. 'But I guess you'd expect that. I just got the feelin' it meant more . . . don't know why or what. And that's about it. The sheriff arrived then. You can ask him what happened next.'

Pease thought for a second, then turned to confront Emple. But before he could say what was on his mind, Niles Stockman stepped into the jailhouse. The Spills rider chinked some coin in his hand, placed it down carefully on Emple's desk.

'Grad's been doin' some figurin' . . . reckons he could be wrong, Sheriff,' he said.

'That'll be a first,' Pease said smartly.

'Yeah, well, he figures you'll be grantin' bail then,' Stockman replied, thinking on Pease's rejoinder. 'This is it . . . ten dollars,' he offered. Then he ran his eyes over Matt and, with the trace of a smirk, made for the open doorway.

As he was about to step on to the boardwalk, Emple yelled at him. 'Not so fast, cowboy.'

Stockman looked back insolently. 'If it ain't enough . . . too bad. Take it up with Grod. I done my bit, Sheriff,' he blustered.

Emple took a couple of steps towards the cowhand. 'What about the charges he made?' he snapped. 'That too bad as well, is it?'

Stockman shrugged. 'Like I said. Grod thinks he coulda been wrong. That's it.' And with that, Stockman was gone.

While Emple stared out into the street, Doc Pease called his name, picked up the cell keys, tossed them to him.

'Well now you got no reason to hold him, Shave. At least you made ten dollars out of it.'

Emple caught the keys, fidgeted with them a few moments, then unlocked Matt's cell.

Matt walked out, collected his gun

from the desk. He checked the cylinder, pushed it into his coat pocket. Then he went back into the cell picked up his hat and, tugging it back on his head, nodded at the sheriff.

'No hard feelin's son.' Emple said. 'I was just doin' my job.'

'I know it,' Matt granted. He nodded at Pease, waited for Emple to say something else.

'There's somethin' I'd like to know . . . get settled,' was what the sheriff asked of him.

'What's that, Sheriff?'

'What you intend to do now.'

'First off I'm goin' to see my horse is OK. Then I'm goin' to get me some rib-stikker, wash it down with a bottle o' whiskey. That'll be white man's, o' course,' he added with a quick look at Pease. 'I need to wash the taste o' this hog-pen out o' my mouth. After that I don't know. I really don't.'

'Yeah, well that's the part I'm interested in. I suggest you keep ridin',' Emple said. 'Mitcham ain't foolin' me by postin' bail. An' I don't want you tanglin' with him.'

'I don't want me tanglin' with him either. But that's up to him,' Matt said, and followed Niles Stockman out on to the street.

Emple took a step forward, but Pease dropped an off-putting hand on his arm. 'Easy there, Shave. You've done your best so far by that boy. Now leave well alone.'

'If he goes down to Scully's, an' Mitcham's there with the others, they'll bust him. Hell, you know that.'

'Yeah, I know it. At least I know they'll try.' Pease's eyes were suitably agleam with the prospect.

Emple noticed, and rumbled an oath. 'Damn you, Harry. You had that in mind when you first came over. You spoke up for that 'breed drifter just to get him back out there . . . back on the street.'

'Time Mitcham was pegged down, Shave. Haven't seen anyone much in the last few months who could do it

. . . not until now. Want to move some checkers . . . fill in the time?'

'Did you see what he did with that fancy bindin' he was wearin' round his middle?'

'Yeah, he wound it up, put it in his pocket.'

'What for? Why'd he do that?'

'Dunno. Perhaps he don't want to get a bullet through it. Why don't you go ask him? You know where he's headed.'

'Yeah, I just might, by Christ. If them gulchers start cuttin' up again, I'll send 'em back to Spills short handed. And Case along with 'em, if he answers their call.'

Pease watched the lawman stamp to his desk. The sheriff buckled his gun belt back on, pushed his pipe into a top pocket, his mouth working away at fitting threats. He knew full well what would happen when Matt Case and Grod Mitcham met up again. He slammed his desk drawer closed and tossed the ring of cell keys at the wall peg, cursed when they missed, clattered on the floor.

Doc Pease went out on to the boardwalk and squinted against the falling sun. He saw Matt draw his horse into the side-street down from Scully's Rooms. He called back to Emple.

'No need to hurry, Shave. Our boy's goin' to where he said. He's lookin' out for that grey o' his.'

Emple pushed some papers into a heap on his desk, and then with a purposeful tug at the brim of his old Stetson, joined Pease on the boardwalk. The doctor pointed to the land west of town where a trail ran in a thin line across the plain. Dust was rising, lifting to make a low cloud between White Basin and Eagle Tail Mountain's timbered slopes.

'Stage's comin' in,' Pease said.

It was late afternoon but heat still shimmered across the land. 'Be here in ten, fifteen minutes,' Emple mumbled.

Pease laughed and stared off across the street. 'Give you somethin' else to worry about,' he called out over his shoulder.

The sheriff waited until Pease had stepped on to the porch of his house at the end of the main street before he closed the door of the jailhouse and turned the key.

★   ★   ★

Matt gave Bull Lome's boy instructions on how to tend his horse, then he went out front to the street.

He stood a moment, listened to the low rolling rumble of wheels and the creak of harness above the day's afternoon stillness. He saw the Yuma coach bumping its way across the hard country, heard the driver yipping at the team in his final dash for town.

He watched some townsfolk emerge from stores, stand expectant along the boardwalks. Not unlike himself, there was no practical reason for them to meet the stage. They simply needed to see, get touched by events and happenings distant from their own isolated frontier town.

Matt turned on his heel, walked towards the saloon. He allowed himself a moment's thought for Grod Mitcham and the sheriff's warning about retaliation. But he was too thankful to be away from confinement to allow time for Mitcham and his colleagues.

He was close to Scully's Rooms when, ahead and to his right, a rider emerged from an alleyway. Matt recognized him as a partner of Grod Mitcham. It was Niles Stockman, one of the two who'd stood back while old Homer Welles was getting himself killed. But the man paid Matt no heed, turned out of the narrow lane and went on along the street.

Matt had stopped walking, took a step back beneath an overhang. But when Stockman went on by, he stepped out again. The noise of the stage had got close, started to swell in the street around him. He stepped up on to a low boardwalk, curious at the stage-coach's arrival. He was amused at how he, too, was caught up in the excitement as people drifted more quickly now towards the depot landing.

It was the break from his inborn watchfulness that made Matt unprepared for the big loop of rope that suddenly dropped over his shoulders. For the briefest moment he was confused, then his hands jerked upwards, took hold of the tightening rope as he heeled about. The drag by the rider in the street wrenched Matt from the boardwalk, but he caught sight of two more men as they rode from the alley-way. He was pulled off balance, was falling when he recognized the leering face of Grad Mitcham, as he heard Shave Emple yell out from somewhere behind him.

As he lost his footing he went down. He turned away, but the side of his face slammed into the hard-packed surface of the street. He sucked in a mouthful of alkali dust, spat and grabbed upwards along the taut line of the rope. But Niles Stockman wheeled his horse and kicked it into a lunging run.

Matt was dragged on his chest for

several yards before a hard-baked runnel turned him over. He went with the movement, got on to his back. For twenty, thirty more yards or so, he drew up his legs, dug his heels and thought quickly.

It was the sort of punishment he knew about, could deal with. He'd heard other tales from his Cree grandfather, Chief Josef Fish, learned how braves had tortured their bodies in testing themselves for strength and visions. But right now, and like a lot of things Indian, Matt only had the legend to go by.

Stockman was getting excited, had started to whoop a bit. Mitcham and another man were riding along the trail of Matt's dust. He twisted over on to his chest again, made a desperate clutch up the rope's length to gain a grip higher up.

He swung his legs around into an arc, pressed his knees into the ground and gave one tremendous jerk. Momentarily the rope slackened and, half-bent,

Matt lumbered to his feet, staggered a few steps. He leaned back against the rope, braced his legs. Then he hauled with all his angered strength. He looked up and, from the middle of the street, saw the stagecoach bearing down on him.

Sheriff Emple was still yelling wildly as he ran forwards. From the edge of his porch, Doc Pease was swearing freely. The town's dog pack was crouched in a semi-circle beneath the boardwalk. Their hackles were raised and they barked madly at the noise and disorder.

Matt saw just about everything fleetingly, before he saw the alarmed eyes of the coach driver. The driver was open-mouthed at what he could see in the road ahead of him. He was dragging frantically on the reins with one hand, the brake lever with the other. Stockman meanwhile had been swung about in his saddle, was trying to control his kicking, frightened mount. Matt jerked again on the rope, dragged the man from his saddle. Then, as the coach veered around him, he moved forward. He pulled the slack rope from his upper body, closed in on the man who was getting up from the ground.

Matt wasted no time. With both hands he grabbed Stockman's lank hair, pulled him upright. 'That's a bad thing you just done to me,' he threatened. He stared into the man's craven eyes. 'What have I ever done to you?'

He hit the man in the stomach with his left hand, pushed his head back down with his right. He brought up his knee sharply, groaned in mutual torment as Stockman's teeth snapped through his tongue. Then he stepped back as the bright blood spurted. The man stared at his boots as the blood dripped, globuled thickly in the dirt between them.

Matt stepped forward again. He chopped swiftly at Stockman's neck with the side of his hand, watched impassively as he went down. 'Now you got an answer,' he affirmed.

5

A Rest For Some

Matt turned to see that the stage had slowed around him. He'd felt the closeness of the big iron-bound hubs as the wheels churned within inches of his lower back. The heavy vehicle had gone on another twenty yards. It tore out the boardwalk railings of White Basin's boarding-house before coming to rest with its near-side door only a few feet off the depot's landing stage. The driver was huffing and puffing, turned to look back at Matt who'd now moved from the centre of the street.

Two young ranch hands were controlling the frightened horses, hanging on to lead traces, while the driver swung himself down from his box. The rear off-side window blind furled open and the face of a young woman looked out. She glanced quickly at Matt and the agitated crowd. Matt saw her push the knuckles of her small fist into her mouth, had time to see the foreboding in her bright eyes.

Then Matt heard the pounding of hooves as a horse bore down on him. He went into a crouch, turned in time to see Grod Mitcham swinging himself from his horse. With one hand the big man was hanging from his saddle horn, ready to launch himself.

Matt braced, then pistoned his legs and raised his hands. As Mitcham crashed down on him, he grabbed at a long leather jerkin. He swung the big man around then let go. He got himself a yard away as Mitcham's shoulder hit the ground. But the man was agile. He rolled with the impact, came up cursing to face Matt.

Matt braced himself as Mitcham came down at him. The man was wild for a fight, lashed out with a flurry of blows. One smashed into the side of Matt's head and he went back on his heels. Then he stepped aside as Mitcham continued to swing at him.

Matt caught two more glancing blows before he regained his balance, then he dipped under a wild swing and brought his clenched knuckles up under Mitcham's jaw. The heavy man was jolted, but he'd set his thick neck, tucked his head in and bunched his shoulder muscles. He took the blow well, and another that Matt shafted in at his meaty face. There was a flat splatter of noise, but again nothing much happened. Mitcham opened up his big arms, broke into Matt's attack with a machinelike ferocity.

As Matt backed off, his senses started working away. As both men fought their way across the street he could see a crowd milling, keeping wide in an expanding circle. He heard Shave Emple yelling and closer, saw Harry Pease staying with the fight.

It was then that Matt knew he had the measure of his opponent. He knew he could take a breath, pick his spot, consider the blow. He almost grinned as he ducked a great looping right, then he stopped, moved quickly forward and drove in a straight right hand to Mitcham's forehead. As the man's head shook he sent in another with the same hand, felt the spasm of pain in the bones of his fingers and wrist as he connected with teeth. Mitcham was done, but he lumbered on. His eyes were glazed and he spat blood, made low guttural noises from his smashed mouth.

'Goddamn you two. Cut it out,' Emple shouted.

Matt heard the sheriff above the clamour of the excited street crowd. But he didn't need to act on it, and Mitcham wasn't going to pay him any heed.

Matt breathed deep, bit his lip at the pain in his forearm. He turned to have a look at the coach, saw the girl still looking from the window. Her eyes met his and he could see the troubled look in her colour-drained face. The stage driver was speaking to her, but her attention had been seized by what she was witnessing in the street.

It was Grod Mitcham, and he'd found the life to come back at Matt. He got close, roared in with both hands around Matt's neck, bent him backwards. Matt brought up the heel of is boot, caught Mitcham full and hard. He felt the man's tough fingers loosen and he spun himself around fast. He was up close to the man's bloodied face and he didn't like it, felt the revulsion. He remembered his pa once telling him it was the big ones that went down hardest, it just took them a bit longer.

Matt wrenched himself free, at the same time jabbed his left hand hard all over Mitcham's face, then his neck. Each time Mitcham's head came straight, he hit him again with a blow to the opposite side of his head. Hard against bone, Mitcham's cheek split open and blood gushed, then an eyebrow was torn.

Both Matt's arms were hurting and

he took a small step back to finish Mitcham off. He half-turned away, swung up his foot, caught Mitcham hard around his back, deep in his kidneys. It was a blow that a one-time Blackfoot friend had taught him many years before. This time it was the end for Mitcham and Matt knew it. He watched with little satisfaction as the big man staggered around in a tight circle.

Mitcham caught sight of the coach and reached out for it. He got his hands on the windowsill, looked up into the terrified face of the girl. She gasped, shrank away and he laughed before his legs gave way and he crumpled heavily to the street.

Matt wiped the blood from the torn skin of his knuckles. His ribs, most of his body, hurt and he breathed in short shallow gasps. But his head cleared and he rubbed at his mouth with his coat sleeve.

He walked slowly towards the coach, was close when Emple angrily pushed two onlookers aside, stepped down from the boardwalk. The gathered crowd had gone silent now, most of the people stood watching Matt. It was the first time they'd seen anything of the like done to Grod Mitcham.

Emple stood in the yellow light of the late afternoon sun.

'OK, son,' he growled. 'We both know he had it comin'. Now move away.'

Matt looked tiredly at the lawman, said nothing. He glanced to the window of the coach saw the girl staring at him, through him. Her lips moved and she shook her head.

Then Doc Pease called out anxiously. 'Look out!'

Both the sheriff and Matt swung around. Matt saw Reefer Chawke reeling along the boardwalk. He was just beyond the coach team, was dragging a leg, his right arm hanging useless at his side. In his outstretched left he gripped a long-barrelled Colt, swung the barrel chillingly at Matt.

'Damn your hide, Chawke. Put the gun down,' Emple yelled.

But Reefer Chawke had come too far to stop. He'd sucked on the laudanum like a newborn. He passed behind the coach and its team, pushed his back up against the wall of the stage-depot building. His eyes were red-rimmed, filled with hopeless loathing as he started squeezing the trigger, holding his aim. He was baring his teeth for the kill when, without hesitation, Matt went for his own Colt. He pulled the gun from his side pocket, actioned off one shot before Chawke had the chance to fire.

The roar split the pall of intense silence in the street. A lady shrieked and the dogs opened up again with their barking. As the echoes rebounded across the town, Matt's bullet hammered high into Chawke's chest. The man couldn't go back, just slid down the clapped wall, sat cross-legged and died. His head lolled forward and the last of the day's light slanted sharp across his shirt front, its shadow partly hiding the spreading stain.

Matt looked at the coach, saw the girl was no longer looking from the window. Mitcham hadn't stirred, but the man who'd thrown the rope was moving forward.

Niles Stockman's vindictive glare drilled into Matt. But the sheriff had been watching him, had seen him rise from the street where Matt had dumped him. He lifted the barrel of his favoured shotgun.

'Don't, Stockman,' he shouted. 'Just get back.'

Stockman thought for a second, then, dribbling bright blood down his chin, he lowered his gunhand.

Matt stepped away from Emple's side.

'They ain't ever goin' to give in, are they, Sheriff?' he said.

Emple swore to himself.

'Like hell they won't. This fight's over,' he stated for the attention of everyone. 'The next man, woman or child who goes for a gun will find themselves laid out on Harry's bench with an ass full o' buckshot, God help me.' He moved towards Chawke, pushed at the body with his boot. 'He must o' wanted this real bad,' he muttered. Then he turned back to Stockman.

'You get Mitcham on his horse . . . get him out o' my sight . . . out o' this town. Tell Spills what happened here. Make sure you tell him as it was. Have him contact any o' Chawke's kin . . . not that they'd own up to it. Stayin' away's a town order, Stockman. It applies to both o' you. Now get out.'

Stockman made sullen noises as he shifted across to Mitcham. He dragged at the big man's clothing but, as a dead weight, Mitcham was too much for him.

'Would you go get their horses?' Emple asked one of the youngsters who'd been holding on to the coach team's harness.

A few minutes later he asked both

lads to fold Mitcham across the saddle of his horse.

'The town'll take care o' Chawke,' he told Stockman when the man had got painfully on to his own horse.

Stockman was still looking bitterly at Matt. He opened his mouth, was going to spit out the last say when Emple snarled at him:

'Remember, you're through here, Stockman. You an' your kind. Now get out an' stay out. Ride!'

Matt stood undaunted and unmoved. He took his waistband from his pocket, thoughtfully looped it around his middle. Stockman had a look at him, then he turned his horse down the street and walked on, led Mitcham's horse behind.

Emple watched silently until Stockman rode to the end of the main street, then he turned to Matt.

'Well what now? You finished the show or what? Perhaps another act to close with?'

'No. I ain't got any more. You saw

what happened,' Matt told him straight.

'Yeah, I saw. The whole goddamn town saw . . . got impressed too. But I'm thinkin' we ain't ideally suited. Perhaps it would be for the best if you rode on as well.'

Matt didn't answer, looked away towards the Eagle Tail Mountains. He thought maybe he *should* ride on, see if he could find which particular part of the country his pa meant him to make *his*.

Emple stepped past him, had another look at Chawke. He asked the two boys to carry the dead cowhand to Bull Lome's livery stable, then he started to get the street cleared, dispersing the crowd.

Harry Pease was now standing outside Scully's. The town doctor was smoking one of his cigarillos, holding a glass of whiskey. Emple stopped close by Pease and, noticing the doctor's satisfaction, he growled:

'There ain't goin' to be any more trouble out here, Harry. So why don't you get off the street, too?'

'All I been doin' is puttin' forward my opinion. The fact that that opinion's evidence, ain't exactly my fault, nor what ensued,' he railed in good humour.

'You interferin' old duffer. Don't try an' soft-soap me,' Emple came back with. 'You an' I both know who was ringleadin' all this.'

Pease shook his head, grinned mischievously as the sheriff started back along the street towards the jail-house.

The stagecoach team was now standing quiet, and the driver had tied off the reins, set the handbrake. He went to the side door and opened it. Almost immediately he called out for the doc.

Pease put down his glass, threw his smoke aside and hurriedly crossed the street. The moment he saw the girl's stockinged legs he shoved the driver out of the way, climbed into the coach. He could see the girl was pale, but she appeared unhurt.

'Sittin' in here ain't ideal for one's constitution,' he called out to Emple, who'd returned to the coach on hearing the driver shout.

'Who is she?' Emple asked the driver.

'Came from Yuma. Name's M. Welles,' said the driver who was craning his neck for a look.

'Welles?' Emple asked.

'M. Welles. That's what it says on the passenger list, an' on the luggage tags,' the driver answered. 'You want that I should help, Doc?'

'No, keep away,' Pease told him. 'Just move her luggage to the depot. I'll send somebody for it later.'

The doc eased the girl to her feet and into Emple's arms, then climbed down.

'We'll take her to my place, poor kid. What a first sight this must've been for her. No wonder she headed for the floor.'

As she came to, the two men helped her across the street, down to the end of town. They made her comfortable on a couch in Pease's front room, then after

Pease lifted a window full open, they went out on to the porch.

'You hear that name, Harry?' Emple asked of the doc.

'Yeah. You don't reckon . . . ?' he said, the question tailing off.

'Don't know. I got other things to take care of,' Emple said. He cast a jaundiced eye up and down the now quiet street. He lifted a hand in acknowledgement, made off to the jailhouse to administer the burying of Reefer Chawke.

Doctor Harry Pease was left muttering the girl's name to himself.

'Welles,' he said. 'Welles. She's got his eyes. It's just got to be . . . goddamnit.'

6

The Hired Hand

'Well, hallo there. You feeling better, young lady?' said Elspeth Barrow.

In response, the girl raised herself from the couch. But Doc Pease's house-keeper and nurse eased her back again.

'You rest up some, honey,' she said. 'You're not comin' to any harm by stayin' right there. Your bags are outside in the hallway an' the doctor's in the next room.'

The girl wanted her bearings, looked around her uneasily. But the warm smile of Elspeth relaxed her a little.

'What happened?' she asked. 'Where am I?'

'Nothing very much happened, except you passed out. You're not hurt. I'll go fetch the doc in, but don't you go bother-in' to get up now.'

Elspeth went off. A minute or so later Pease came in. He sat at the girl's feet, at the end of the couch. He took her wrist, checked her pulse-rate.

'As I thought,' he said. 'You're goin' to live. I'm Harry Pease, but you can call me Doc. You just passed out. I'm guessin it was the heat. It was a charnel house inside that coach.'

'No, it wasn't that,' the girl said, taking her hand back from Pease's. 'It was that man's face. It was so close . . . so horrible.'

'Yeah, I know what you mean. Ain't a pretty sight at the best o' times. It was regrettable that you had to get such a front seat. Miss Welles, isn't it?'

'Yes. Matilda Welles,' the girl said. 'But you can call me Tilly,' she added, with a glint in her eye. 'I came here from Prescott. I got on the coach at Yuma, but I guess you already know that. I'm seeking my uncle Homer. You'll probably know him, Doctor. Homer Welles?'

Pease turned slightly away. His brow

creased and he swallowed hard because he'd guessed right.

'Is there something wrong?' Tilly asked. 'Dr Pease?'

Pease delayed another moment before turning. His face was drawn tight and his eyes looked heavy under his grey brows. He nodded slowly, turned to face her.

'Yes, there is something wrong,' he said. 'Your uncle's dead. Matilda . . . Tilly. He was killed today . . . just today. It was in town. There was another fight. I'm real sorry.'

Tilly shook her head, unbelieving.

'Another fight?' she asked, her voice thin and incredulous.

'Yes. What you saw in the street . . . that was the aftermath of it, I guess. The one that's dead . . . he's the one . . . the one that — '

'The one that killed my uncle,' Tilly said, finishing the doc's sentence for him.

Pease nodded. 'I am very sorry,' he said. 'Homer was a friend as well as a patient. Not close, but a friend nevertheless. I know he was a good man. There's more than a few people in this town who did know him well . . . will miss him. Not one of 'em could o' stopped what happened, though.'

'What did happen, Doctor?'

'He got involved in an argument with some cowhands from out o' town. Seems like Homer went for his gun. He was killed for doing it.'

'How many of them did it take?' Tilly asked, the hurt and frailty obvious in her voice.

'Just the one,' Pease said quietly.

Tilly blinked the wetness from her eyes, bit her lip.

'I wanted to tell him . . . ask him if I could help. There was nothing left for me up north.' There was a short silence, then she added, 'Not like down here.'

Pease watched her in silence, felt the acid scorn. He was unable to come up with words to make sense of it; her arrival in town, the timing. After leaving the room he closed the door quietly after him, hoped she'd understand. He asked Elspeth to look after her, somehow keep her in the house for a while.

He went down to Scully's then, ordered himself a beer and whiskey-chaser. Matt Case was standing at the end of the counter with Shave Emple and he got a round for them too. He held the beer in his right hand, pushed the whiskeys along the counter with his left.

'The girl's Homer's niece. I think she'll be stayin' for a while.'

'His niece eh? I did wonder on it. She's come a long way to find him dead,' the sheriff said, almost resentful.

'Yeah, ain't that the hell of it,' Pease agreed. 'She can't be no more'n twenty, an' all I can do is take her pulse, an' tell her what a lot of friends Homer had in town. What sort o' prattle-gob does that make me, eh?'

Matt studied the old doctor's face. 'You talkin' about the girl in the stage?' he asked.

'Yeah. I reckon she saw all o' that fight . . . that street show you put on out there. That's why she blacked out . . . the horror of it all. An' who's to blame her? From Prescott, she's likely seen nothin' more brutal than somebody squishin' a grasshopper.'

Matt remembered the girl clearly, her white face, grey-green eyes. He felt a strange attraction. They'd both come a long way to White Basin and they'd both lost family. He smiled sparingly, nodded his thanks to Pease for the drink.

Emple studied the whiskey that Pease had stood him.

'It's a sad story, sure enough, but that's about all it is, eh, Doc? I don't see what we can do about it. Besides, I've got other stuff to take care of.'

The doc gave him the beady eye. 'Oh yeah,' he said. 'You got paperwork for a burial to take care of. Most wearisome.'

'No, I've taken care o' that. I'm talkin' about young Matt here.'

'I don't need no lookin' after,' Matt

71

told him with good humour.

The sheriff flicked a shrewd eye at the doc.

'Oh yes you do, son. Oh yes you do,' he said. 'Tell him Harry. Tell him what Grod Mitcham'll do when he gets his senses back.'

'He'll rant some, make threats, get his drawers twisted,' Pease mumbled casually.

'He'll buckle on his gunbelt, that's what he'll do, goddamnit,' Emple snapped. 'He's soaked up a punishment here in town today, an' that's public humiliation for Mitcham . . . for anyone. He ramrods the biggest spread in the territory and keeps the hands in check 'cause they're scared of him . . . scared to hell. As sure as water flows in the Colorado, he'll be back to save his face.'

The sheriff turned to Matt, poked him in the chest.

'He'll come to town lookin' for you, an' it won't be to shoot the breeze. Now, you're short in this town, son. So you just sup that whiskey an' get that nice lookin' grey saddled. You hear me?'

'I hear you, Sheriff,' Matt told him.

Doc Pease looked on, curious. 'Where you headed for?' he asked Matt.

'I don't remember sayin' I was headed anywhere,' Matt said, again with the good-humoured smile.

Emple cracked the base of his glass on the counter.

'Maybe you was too good for Chawke, son. But Grod Mitcham with a gun's another proposition. I told you, he won't be lookin' to do you any favours. He's cunnin'. We'll never know he's there, 'til it's too late. You'll never know. I also told you, I don't want any more trouble in town. Not while I'm still sheriff.'

'There's half o' me that makes it difficult for a man like Mitcham to gain much of an advantage, Sheriff,' Matt said.

'Yeah, an' I bet I know which half,' the doc added.

'A man shouldn't have to ride from

anywhere for no reason,' Matt continued.

Emple was getting exasperated.

'You got a reason. I'm tellin' you . . . ain't askin',' he told Matt shortly.

Doc Pease saw the expression that set Matt's face, hardened his eyes. He was reminded again of the first time he'd seen the man ride into town. Since then, Matt Case had bested Grod Mitcham and three of his cowboy cronies in a side-street. Later, set upon by three of them, he'd got out of Stockman's roping, given Mitcham another beating and shot Reefer Chawke dead. Pease knew his instincts were right about Matthew Case. It was the Cree part that troubled him: the part that had retied the beaded waistband, he noticed.

'I rode hundreds o' miles to reach White Basin, Sheriff,' Matt said. 'It's my pa's homeland, an' he wanted me to see it. So far I can't see the attraction, but I promised him I'd have a look. Now you or anyone else ain't goin' to change that. I've done nothin' wrong.'

'Listen to me, son. Maybe you're right, maybe you ain't done nothin' wrong. But all you're goin' to do is create trouble by stayin' around. Let's face it, you ain't even got yourself a pot to piss in. Your only board was my jail. So, as it is . . . ?'

'As it is, you best hitch up, Shave,' Pease said. 'The boy's not so much a drifter as you might think.'

'Stay out o' this, Harry. Truth be told, you caused both of us enough trouble today already.'

'Can't do that, Shave. Wouldn't be fair on Matt.'

'What the hell you jabberin' on about?' the sheriff demanded, looked quizzically at Matt.

'He's got himself work,' Pease said. 'The Welles girl needs help out at Homer's place. At least 'til probate's done. I suggested she takes on Matt.'

Emple's jaw dropped. He indicated for the bartender to pour them another round of whiskeys. 'You jobbin' me?' he asked, having taken a moment to grasp what the doc had said.

Pease ran some coin on to the counter for the whiskeys.

'No I'm serious. I came lookin' for him. They got things to discuss . . . him an' Miss Welles. You don't think I came in here for your company do you, you old wooser.'

'You probably thought, here's where the next load o'trouble's comin' from,' Emple grumbled.

The doc studied his whiskey. 'Seems to me, you could be a tad more appreciative, Shave. Maybe get the town to award him one o' them civil-duty badges. Chawke ain't goin' to be missed, an' he handed Mitcham nothin' more'n he's been askin' for for a long time. You tell me what's so wrong with that?' Pease nodded, continued with his zeal. 'Look at it from the girl's point o' view. She gets here to find herself in the middle of a gunfight . . . finds out her uncle's been shot dead . . . an' she's no one to turn to. So puttin' young Matt to work ain't such a daft idea. That trouble you, eh, Shave?'

'Homer's land rests smackbang up against the Spills spread. In case it slipped your mind, Grod Mitcham ramrods it. Does that trouble me? You out of your mind?'

Doc Pease grinned. 'Yeah. Good ain't it?' he said, with a roguish twinkle in his eye.

'By hell! I could probably get you for disturbin' the peace or somethin' similar . . . toss you in a cell even, for that,' Emple retorted.

'Do nobody any good, Shave. Least of all Egan Dartmouth and his waterbelly trouble. The Mutton woman's expectin' to drop another child any day, an' Ma — '

'Gaaargh,' Emple said. He picked up his drink, finished it in one gulp. 'To hell with everybody. Don't know why I bother to even *try* an' keep the peace in this hell-hole.' He glowered at Matt, then back to Pease. 'I'll be glad when they call time on this day.' Then the sheriff coughed, wiped his chin and walked dourly from the saloon.

Pease raised his eyebrows, took a sip at the remainder of his drink.

'I know what you're thinkin', son. I'm ready when you are,' he said to Matt, who was still looking at him enquiringly.

Matt finished his drink. 'Is that the truth . . . what you just told the sheriff?' he asked.

Pease grinned some. 'The idea of it was, I got the notion you want to stick around. Sheriff Emple or Grod Mitcham notwithstandin'?'

Matt raised his chin, studied the doctor.

'If that means what I think it means, yeah. I need some more time here . . . roundabouts.'

'You lookin' for somethin' particular?' Pease asked.

'Don't rightly know,' Matt said warily but honest. 'Did you know that girl . . . before today?'

'Matilda Welles? No never seen her before. I'm not so sure old Homer had either. I guess he woulda said some-thin'.' Pease was thoughtful for a few seconds, then he said, 'I got myself involved now . . . so I got to do somethin' to help. If what those Spills men — '

'Hey. Hold up a second, Doc,' Matt interrupted him. 'You ropin' me in? You got somethin' else on your mind other than me bein' white girl's hoe man?'

'Maybe, son. Maybe.' Pease said, smiling uneasily at Matt's belittling turn of phrase.

Matt made a twisted grin, shook his head. 'Then it's no deal. I can find enough trouble by just mindin' my own business.'

'You're in too deep for the luxury of gettin' by on that, son. An' I've seen enough to know that runnin' scared don't figure much in your life. So why not help out the Welles girl, while you're waitin' up? Mitcham's comin' for you anyways.'

Matt knew that some of what the doc said was true. He turned to the back bar, stared thoughtfully at the labels on the bottles of drink.

'I don't know quite why I came here,' he said, 'but I know it weren't for this.'

Pease leaned across the counter, stood very close. 'Hell, Matt. If you want to look the ground over, what you got to lose? No one else is goin' to employ you. They're too goddamn scared.'

Matt wiped a hand tiredly across his brow.

'She sure had a nice face . . . Matilda Welles. Her eyes were the same colour as her uncle's. I noticed that,' he said with some thought.

Pease agreed. 'Yep, an' Homer was a good ol' stick by all accounts. Wouldn'ta stole a hair from the back o' one o' them mad dogs out front. An' from what you say, Matt, he was killed sayin' just that. You went to help him; weren't your fault that things got out o' hand an' he got shot dead, was it?'

'No, it wasn't,' Matt said falteringly. He wondered whether in some curious way, the doc was implicating him, putting some guilt his way.

'That's right,' Pease confirmed. 'What's more, you can't just walk away, can you, as if nothin's happened? There's too much molasses stickin' to your legs for that, son.'

Matt gave a few Red River trapper curses, looked resignedly around him. He knew full well that during the next few days, he would have to consider his next move. Tiresome. Most of his anguish would be caused by those who wanted to get close, side with the town's new champion. But he was a man unused to the press of a crowd, the brush of sudden notoriety.

'Let's go see Miss Welles, then,' he said. 'I guess I owe her, 'specially if I'm to blame for the horror of it all,' he added ironically.

'Fine. That's just fine,' beamed a satisfied Doc Pease. And before Matt could change his mind, he led the way from the saloon.

7

First Dark

Harry Pease led the way into his house.
But he stopped just inside the door, saw
Elspeth Barrow was waiting for him,
her face tight with anxiety.

Pease looked towards the closed door
of his front room.

'How is she?' he asked.

'Poorly. I don't think she's takin' it
well,' Elspeth replied. 'I don't think it's
my sort of nursin' she's after. She just
lyin' there, staring into space.'

Pease puffed out his cheeks, fiddled
with the cigarillos in his coat pocket.
'Leave it to me then,' he said. 'Not that
it's my doctorin' she needs either. You
better light some more lamps before
you get dinner ready, Elspeth. We'll eat
early. eh? Perhaps the smell o' meat
juices'll bring her round. She may well

think o' leavin' after she's more settled, got some food inside her.'

'Oh, I don't think so, Doctor. It's almost full dark now. Where'll she be goin' in an hour or so?' Elspeth said, the concern evident in her voice.

'Take a seat. I won't be a minute,' Pease said to Matt. 'I'll go an' see her, find out what she's thinkin'.'

Pease knocked on the door of the room where the girl was resting. But there was no response. He opened the door gently and went in.

Tilly Welles was sitting up, wedged at the rising end of the couch. She was clasping her hands together, eyes unresponsive as she faced Pease's concern. He could see she'd hardly moved. He took a couple of paces towards her, but she held up a hand that meant she wasn't yet ready.

'Yeah. I know. I'm sorry,' he said sympathetically. 'Not the sort o' thing you recover from in a couple of hours. I'll leave you for a bit. You know we're here.

Pease backed off, watched her for a moment further, then closed the door quietly. He rejoined Matt in the other room.

'I don't think she's too interested in talkin' cattle grubs,' he said. 'An' who's to blame her. Guess I'll just have to carry on makin' decisions.'

Matt stood, pondered on what the old doctor was saying. You make the decisions, I'll do the fighting, he thought. He had the distinct feeling that Pease had wheedled him into a place he didn't want to be.

'You got entitlement to do that, Doc?' he asked carefully.

'I got a conscience,' Pease said firmly, 'You'll learn that that's a good pillow, son . . . music at midnight. You tell me what you or anyone else should do in the circumstances, an' I'll listen.' He crossed to a desk in the corner of the room and pulled out paper and pencil, sketched a rough map of some country to the north-west of White Basin. 'Here, this is your ticket out o' trouble. Take a ride, go on out and let some air into the place,' he said handing it to Matt. 'Don't know whether Homer locked the place up. He didn't have much on him . . . no keys. Have a look around, do anythin' you figure needs doin'. As soon as the girl's well enough to travel, I'll bring her out.'

'An' if I have visitors?' Matt asked.

Doc Pease gave a slight shrug. 'Well if it ain't me, it'll be the bad guys. Then you fill the place with gunsmoke. Seriously, Matt, I guess you *can* expect visitors. But you'll get 'em anyway, whether you stay in town or find yourself a hole in a wall somewhere. An' remember, it's probably the only way Shave Emple's goin' to let you stick around these parts. Right?'

Matt shrugged. It wasn't quite the answer he was hoping for or expecting. He thought back to when he'd told the doc he wasn't sure what he was looking for, what he wanted in White Basin. That's when he'd lost his way and he knew it, but it was too late now. He picked up his hat.

'How far's this place, then?' he asked.

The doc pointed to the map he'd sketched. 'It's a ways. Take you best part of three hours, I reckon. Keep Stand Up Rock ahead o' you, steer just north of east. You'll ford the Dog Creek twice, the second time head west. Can't miss the place.'

As Matt walked to the door, Elspeth came out and smiled politely.

'Will that be another place for dinner?' she asked Pease.

'No, no, he's in a hurry,' said Pease. The response was a little quick to Matt's way of thinking, so he gave Elspeth a wounded smile and stepped out on to the porch. He heard the desert crickets and smelled the night blossoms, took a deep breath. In darkness, the town looked less bleak, less faded with decay. Night-time created an illusory cloak, had the advantage of making places like White Basin look no worse than anywhere else.

He crossed the street, went back to

Scully's Rooms. He indicated a bottle of forty-rod whiskey from the shelf along the backbar, paid the barkeep four dollars. He remembered hearing Chief Josef Fish once tell his father 'whiskey make rabbit hug bear'. He smiled favourably at his grandfather's saw, wondered what would happen if he had a drink with Grod Mitcham. He left the saloon and turned into the side-street, doubtfully made his way to Bull Lome's livery.

He gave the stable boy a dollar, led his grey out front and saddled it. Five minutes later and, still uncertain if he was right, wrong, wise or foolish, he rode out into the main street, headed west at the end of town.

* * *

Doc Pease slumped in his deckchair, heaved a long sigh of relief. Elspeth Barrow leaned against the porch rail, studied him closely as he lit one of his cigarillos.

'Are you goin' to tell me what you're up to?' she said.

'I'm not up to anything,' he replied, with a barely visible shake of his head.

'Oh, yes you are, Doc. I've known you too long not to know when there's something devious going on in that head o' yours. Gosh, the countless hours I've spent listenin' to men's deliriums, their never-to-be realized imaginin's. I recognize the look. Nine times out of ten there was a woman involved. You're not the only one concerned about the girl, you know.'

'Those men you're talkin' of were dyin' Elspeth. They needed those imaginin's. With 'em, they knew they were still livin'. Anyways, I got us into this problem, it's up to me to get us out . . . me an' Tilly Welles, that is. You stick to lookin' after my patients an' the house, Elspeth. Leave the other stuff to me.'

'Hmm. I'll wager it's the 'other stuff' that's got you into whatever trouble you're talkin' about,' Elspeth continued with her concerns. 'You're involved in something you should've stayed away from, or someone.'

'What *are* you goin' on about, Elspeth?'

'The Spills foreman, Grod Mitcham. He's obviously no match for that young man ... Matthew Case, but to a silly, meddlin' old sawbones? Tell me you're not involved in somethin' you shouldn't be, Doc ... please,' Elspeth caringly demanded.

'You reckon I should let her ride out to Homer's place on her own?' Pease said, veering away from Elspeth's question. 'You saw how distraught she was when we brought her in, didn't you? Good God, Elspeth, she fainted at the sight of Mitcham gettin' himself a fat lip.'

'Yes, I saw.' Elspeth said. 'And I can see how you'd want to help her. You're bored, tired of something, Doc, and you want some excitement. But you're confusin' that with trouble ... big trouble.'

Pease watched Elspeth walk away. But he knew he could depend on her. He'd known it from the time they'd walked from the carnage of war, decided to travel west. It was at Chickamauga that they'd first met, when she'd worked alongside the field surgeons as a volunteer nurse.

Moving off the porch, Pease walked across his small front yard. Tilly Welles had remained in his front room, hadn't shown any inclination to leave the house or even talk to anyone. Not that that bothered the doc. It was getting justice for Homer Welles, getting punishment with the Coomer Spills hands, that did that. And to that end, he wanted Matt Case out on the Welles place.

He stood by his picket fence, considered another smoke, but took a few breaths of the cool night air. Looking at the lights along the main street he heard wild shouts from inside and outside Scully's Rooms. He thought about the old days when towns like

White Basin had been open, neighbourly places with no man or family down on their luck, no man as wealthy and dangerously influential as Coomer Spills.

He considered the trouble he'd caused Shave Emple, decided to take a stroll to the jailhouse. The sheriff was sitting moodily at his desk, building a low stockade with shotgun cartridges. Pease grunted a welcome and pulled the checker board from under Emple's hat, arranged the well-worn pieces.

Emple challenged him with a look, watched him make the first move on the board.

'OK,' he said, 'a whiskey a game,' and went for his pipe.

'Two,' said the old doctor and leaned over the board with eager resolve.

★　★　★

'So much for the early dinner,' Elspeth said, when Doc Pease returned two hours later.

'Yeah, sorry, Elspeth. I got caught up

91

winnin' me a half-bottle of whiskey,' he said, unbuttoning his coat.

'Well, while you've been doing that, Tilly's got herself up and about. She's asking for you. Looks like she's shook off the worst.'

The doc looked pleased and went to the door of his front room, but Elspeth told him the girl was at the rear of the house. He found Tilly sitting at the kitchen table. She had a bowl of broth, untasted and cooling before her. She looked up when he came in and gave him a reserved smile.

'I'm sorry for the trouble I've caused you. Elspeth made this for me, but I can't — ' she was saying. But Pease interrupted, drawing up a chair.

'Appetite'll come with the first mouthful,' he advised, 'an' it's no trouble. I don't do much that I don't want to any more. An' if there *is* any trouble, believe me, it ain't started yet.'

'Hmm,' Tilly said, not picking up on Pease's forewarning. 'My uncle told me very little about the town or his life here. After Pa's death he just wrote and said to come on out. It took me nearly three months to tidy up Pa's affairs, though.'

'You lost your pa as well?' Doc asked, grimacing.

Tilly bit her lip and nodded, gave the broth a stir.

The doctor gave her wrist a short, understanding grasp. 'If there's any truth in trouble comin' three times, you've certainly had your share, young lady,' he said thoughtfully. 'I do know that sometimes you got to face up to these things . . . meet 'em head on. So, why not stay . . . open a new chapter in your life . . . start anew, eh?'

Tilly looked intent. 'How can I? What am I supposed to do? I don't have the money or the knowledge to go into business. I wouldn't know where to start.'

'You know nothin' of ranch work?' Doc asked.

Tilly shook her head. 'I ordered some mail-order seeds once. My pa . . . family ran a shop, a drapers'.'

'I see. Well, it ain't all that challengin'

if you've got a head on you, and an expert hand,' the doc said supportively. 'Homer had himself a decent spread. It's three hours west of here, not big, but the land's pretty. There's good water an' fat grass on the slopes. I'd say there was some ... er ... civic improvements needed, but you ain't inherited a pig in a poke, Tilly.'

'I told you, my background's frills and furbelows. And I'm frightened of horses and cattle. They've always scared the wits out of me ... big ugly brutes.'

'In a lot o' ways, cattle an' horses are about the same as people out here, Tilly. You treat 'em right ... appeal to their basic instincts, an' they'll line up for you.' Pease went to his top pocket for a cigarillo but changed his mind.

'You can smoke if you want. I don't mind, I'm used to it,' Tilly said.

'No, it's all right. Anyway, Elspeth don't like it.' He patted her arm reassuringly. 'Anyway, your problem ain't so great,' he said, with a little nervous grin. 'I've sent a man out to look after things. He's a rough diamond but there's a charm about him. He won't let you down either.'

'He's the hand, is he?' Tilly asked.

'Yeah. You'll need someone to keep the fences in order . . . chop wood . . . do some roundup an' brandin' work. You know, that sort o' thing.'

'I can only guess, I'm afraid. You've been so kind, I — '

But Pease wouldn't hear the gratitude and he interrupted again. 'I don't know much about Homer's finances,' he said. 'But he never had any loans that I know of. Well, nothin' big enough to cause him any hardship. As I said, the place is probably run down a bit, but I reckon he was makin' out fair enough. You won't have much to worry about there, I'm sure.'

Tilly slowly took a mouthful of chicken broth, supped wistfully. Pease coughed, rose from the table. He thought he'd have been tempted by the girl, a few years ago. But he had Elspeth, so it would have been nothing more.

He was relieved that Tilly hadn't asked him who it was he'd sent out to the ranch.

'I'd like for you to stay here the night,' he said. 'In fact, as your doctor, I'd prescribe it. Then sometime tomorrow we'll see what the bank's got him down for, eh? See if there's any more surprises for you. Maybe the day after, we can ride out and you can see what you've become the owner of.'

Tilly put the spoon back in the bowl and Pease knew he was getting ahead of himself, had said too much. But he thought it a good sign that she didn't appear to be interested in any gain from her uncle Homer's death.

He bade her goodnight, then went back to the porch out front. He drew out the smoke he'd been wanting, listened to the breeze soughing through agave. As his belly grumbled he inhaled deeply, hoped that out of the debris of one long day, a better morning would follow.

8

The Recovery

'You bring him closer, so that I can get a good look at him,' barked Coomer Spills as he stamped down off his veranda to glare at Niles Stockman.

Ever since Clem Rollo had reported back to him about the trouble in town, Spills had been keen to learn more of Homer Welles's killing. The old man had held out on him on a section of land which spiked upwards into his already vast range. Spills had therefore considered his neighbour to be little more than an irksome sodbuster.

Stockman attempted to hold the reins as Mitcham climbed from his saddle and got a kick for it. Then he offered to assist him to the house.

'Get your ham fists off me,' Mitcham said, roughly shoving him away. The big man braced himself on unsteady legs, took a step on to the broad veranda. He gave Stockman a rich curse and brushed past him up into the house. Spills opened his mouth, was on the verge of shouting his man down, when he saw the extent of Mitcham's beating. He sucked in his breath at the overall bruising across the face, the raw, puffed-up mouth and the bloodied nose.

Mitcham went on into the house, so Spills turned on Stockman.

'What the hell happened? He run into the Pacific Flyer?'

'I'll let him tell it,' Stockman said thickly, and led the two horses off. But he'd not got far when Spills shouted after him.

'Hold up, Niles. Where's Reefer?'

'He can tell you that as well,' Stockman spluttered over his shoulder.

'I'm askin' you, goddamnit,' Spills rasped at the truculent ranch hand.

'He's dead. Now, if you don't mind, Mr Spills, my mouth feels like it's got a burnin' log in it, an' I'm kind o' tired. All in all, it's been one hell of a day.'

He started off again towards the corral and Spills glared furiously after him. He was about to shout again, but thought better of it. Instead he hurried into the big day room, to find Mitcham standing with his back to the wall and a glass of Kentucky bourbon in his hand.

'I'm so sorry, Grod,' Spills remarked acidly. 'That was thoughtless o' me. I should o' said make yourself at home, pour yourself somethin' from my liquor cupboard.' Warily, the rancher eyed his foreman. 'Stockman says for you to tell me what happened. So tell me,' he said. 'Clem came back with talk about Reefer killin' Welles. He said there wasn't any trouble with Shave Emple or any other townfolk. Tell me that's true, Grod.'

'It's true,' Mitcham said bluntly.

Spills strode across the room, filled himself a glass of the bourbon and turned back to Mitcham. 'You have anythin' to do with the Welles's killin'?' he challenged.

'Some.'

'You give me no more'n a grunt Grod, an' you'll be no more'n a range bum in these parts,' Spills threatened.

Mitcham pushed himself away from the wall he was leaning against. He took a deep, laboured breath. 'You already been told. It was Reefer shot the old man,' he mumbled. 'Emple couldn't do much about it. But what you don't know is that while we was talkin' to Welles about him rustlin' your beeves — '

'What? What do you mean, rustlin' my beeves?' Spills barked.

Mitcham raised his eyebrows, made a pained expression. 'Yeah. We followed the sign. He had a herd of thirty-five, forty steers. They were bunched in a pole corral at the bottom of the south slope of his spread. We caught up with him in town . . . asked him about it. I figure he panicked . . . went for his gun.'

'Who was it did the askin'?' Spills asked.

'Me.'

Spills swore violently. 'Why the hell didn't you ride back here. You know how I feel about cattle-stealin'. This far from town we practically got lynch law, you know that. I do my own justice.'

'There weren't time, Coomer,' Mitcham said. 'If that sign had worn . . . got windblown, there'd be no proof. Anyways, I only meant to rough him up a bit, get him to squawk his guilt.'

Spills shook his head, slow and incredulous. 'He do that to you, Grod? He give you that beatin?' Spills asked, holding out his glass to indicate the man's damaged face.

Mitcham snorted in his throat, held the back of a hand tentatively under his nose. 'No, it weren't Welles. That was someone called Case. Matthew Case.'

'Case. Who the hell's he?'

'A drifter. He happened by, bought himself in. He got the drop on me . . . got stuck in before I could get myself together.'

'Yeah, an' Reefer?'

'He killed him. Case killed him.'

Spills gaped. 'I don't think I'm wantin' to know the whole o' this story, Grod. But you're tellin' me that Niles, you an' Reefer got jumped by a drifter who just happened by?' he cracked.

'I said, he got the drop on me . . . us. He ain't no normal drifter, either. Not the kind we see in these parts. He looked like he was a . . . I dunno, a 'breed maybe. Mean eyes . . . cold-blooded. I was goin' after him, but Emple stepped in. But no matter, I'll fix him, soon as I'm right in the saddle again.'

'I'm sure you will, Grod,' growled Spills, and Mitcham's eyes narrowed in resentment.

'You ease off, Coomer,' he said flatly. 'You weren't there. You don't know how it was set up. We got your goddamn beeves back, and another rustler's kickin' up brush. As soon as I can, I'm goin' after this Matthew Case.'

'When?' Spills asked.

'I figure, sun-up tomorrow. I'll get a slab o' meat an' some salt on these wounds. Only this time, I won't be involved in any ringster stuff. I'm talkin' lead.'

Spills finished his drink. He put down his glass heavily, signalling their talk was over.

'Yeah, you do whatever you think's best, Grod. I'm kind o' curious. Think I'll take a ride in to town . . . see the sheriff. Find out what's goin' on . . . what Shave's up to.'

Mitcham finished his drink, walked tiredly across the room. He stopped near the open door.

'No, Coomer,' he said with an edge of unease. 'Leave it to me. I know what to do . . . who to do it to. That's what you pay me for. Shouldn't take me more'n a day.'

Spills nodded, followed Mitcham on to the veranda. He'd seen many men who'd been beaten in fights before. Some of it in a mirror when he was making his mark in White Basin. So he knew Mitcham had been hurt bad, wondered about the man calling himself Matthew Case.

Mitcham went across the yard and entered the barn. He found Niles Stockman brushing his horse.

'I told Spills that Case got the drop on me,' he said.

Stockman stopped brushing, looked compliantly at Mitcham. 'That's right, Grod. I mean, there's no one goin' to believe otherwise, is there? An' if that's how you want it to be told . . . ?'

'It is. First thing, you and Clem get to that low country an' clean it out. Take them beeves down to the wash and leave 'em there. They won't go far.'

'What about you?' Stockman asked anxiously.

'I got somethin' to attend to. I ain't lettin' no drifter beat the stuffin' out o' me an' walk away. You just tell the men we was jumped . . . never had a chance. You hear me, Niles?'

'Yeah, an' I got the picture, boss,' Stockman said as Mitcham went back across the yard to the kitchen.

Stockman sneezed, wiped a line of sweat from his forehead. He was troubled, because for the first time since he'd teamed up with Grod Mitcham, they were being bettered. Even Mitcham was shaky, afeared even. He finished up in the barn, let the horses into the night corral and went off to find Clem Rollo.

9

Every Which Way

Sunlight reached the town, sought the blistered surfaces of its clapboard walls, broke the dullness of alleys and side-streets. Eventually, White Basin was only a mere ugly yellow break away from the timbered greenness that bent around the Eagle Tail Mountains.

An outcast from the dog-pack lay in the dust. It panted slightly and rose on its front legs, too uncomfortable to stay in the rising sun. But it fell back again, too lazy to move out of it. A rider came along the main street, threw a package into the doorway of the boarding-house and rode on. A storekeeper swept the litter of his shop on to the boardwalk. On the steps of Scully's Rooms, a grizzled old man sat. He was half-keeled over, not quite fallen and he had both eyes shut. In the narrow street alongside, a woman threw a pail of water over the Bull Lome livery stable sign.

Sitting on his porch, Doc Pease saw Grod Mitcham making his way up the street. When he passed Scully's, and headed on towards the north end of town, the doc eased himself from his deckchair and walked to his front gate. He made his way hurriedly along the boardwalks until he reached the side-street where Homer Welles had met his death. Mitcham was only fifty or so yards ahead of him then and still riding slowly.

Pease turned into the lane and ran in a staggered loop through sheds and workshops until he came to the rear door of the jailhouse. He thumped on the heavy slabs of pine, called for the sheriff.

'Shave. It's me, Harry. Open up, I got somethin' to tell you.'

The door creaked open a few moments later and Emple frowned out at him. The doc didn't bother to make his way into the jailhouse, just said urgently:

'Mitcham's ridin' in. He's comin' this way, an' I reckon we know what for.'

Shave Emple squeezed his eyes shut for a troubled moment.

'Hold up, Harry,' he started, but Pease cut him short.

'He's almost here, Shave. Shut up an' listen to me, will you? I got young Matt Case to ride out to the Welles spread. Someone's got to be there, if only to protect the girl . . . Tilly. There's likely to be trouble, we know that. I been mullin' over what Mitcham an' them cowhands had to say about Homer stealin' their cows. Well, that ain't so . . . can't be. So, who was it moved those cattle on to his land, eh? Who was it gave Mitcham the chance to make the accusation?'

'How the hell would I know?' Emple rumbled impatiently. 'An' how come you got so involved? You said he's here,' so make your point, Harry.'

'Never mind me . . . my involvement, that ain't important. What I'm sayin' is, if it weren't Homer, who was it? But right now, even that don't matter. You got to get us time, Shave. You got to get Case some time.'

The sheriff's brows arched and he puffed, tugged at his loose belt. 'What in blazes you up to, Doc? Time . . . what the hell you want *time* for? By Big Lucy, if you're puttin' those goddamn boots o' yours into — '

Pease banged the flat of one hand against the door-frame.

'I said to listen, Shave. Mitcham must be just pullin' up outside right now. Whatever you say, don't let on where Case has gone. I got a bad feelin' it matters . . . that we all need time. There's somethin' real damn wrong about Homer gettin' shot, the way he was. An' for what it's worth, it ain't my boots, my nose, hands or anythin' else that's leadin' me around. Just tell Mitcham that Matt Case went on his way. Just leave it at that.'

Both men heard the pounding on the front door of the jailhouse. Pease nodded his urgent encouragement at Emple. 'Please, Shave,' he said. 'Just do it.' Then he pushed the back door to before Emple could argue further.

Inside his jailhouse, the sheriff swore and stuffed the tail of his shirt into his pants, tugged at his belt again. He unlocked the front door to let in the Spills foreman.

In the bright, slanting light, Mitcham's face looked a lot worse than he remembered from the day before, had matured badly. His left eye was almost closed, the flesh across his cheeks, his mouth and nose, was deeply coloured and swollen.

'What do you want, Mitcham?' Emple asked.

'Case,' the Spills ramrod said. 'You can back him or me, don't matter much. Just find him . . . tell him.'

'Ride away, Mitcham, before I get lawful. Bustin' in here with your threats an' demands. Who the hell do you think you are?'

'The man who's come for Case,' Mitcham told him thickly. 'You just stay out o' my way, Sheriff. This is between me an' him.'

'Seems like most folk now are tellin' me what to do,' Emple snapped back. 'Shame I'm such an ornery old cuss.' He reached for his gunbelt and buckled it around his spreading middle. Then he pushed past Mitcham, went to sluice water over his face in a corner basin. 'Wouldn't you just love to do this,' he said, towelling himself roughly. 'Now, why don't you just settle down? You asked for everythin' you got, Mitcham.'

'I came lookin' for Case, Emple. Either you go get him or I find him myself. Either way you'll be buryin' him.'

Emple hung the towel on a peg, put his hat on. He smiled thinly.

'You considered that maybe you ain't up to takin' him, Mitcham?' he asked.

Mitcham swore, drew his gun in a

fast, smooth motion and actioned the hammer.

Emple's gunhand dropped instinctively, but he left his gun holstered.

'Jeesus, you should be millin' with them stolen cows, Mitcham. You think a quick draw's enough to kill Matthew Case . . . any man? You really are more stupid than you look, an' that's sayin' somethin'.'

'I was on the ground if you remember. He jumped me from behind. That's how he managed to take me.'

Emple stared at him.

'Rubbish. You came at him like a riled greenhorn. He stepped away, came back an' beat you to a pulp. *That*'s how it was.'

Mitcham released the hammer of his Colt. With both eyes narrowed, he stood rigid with indignation before the lawman.

'I'm sick o' talkin',' he said. 'I want Case, so if you want to see it done fair, you best lead the way, Sheriff.'

'I ain't leadin' you anywhere. There's

no point,' Emple said easily.

Mitcham looked more intently at him. 'You're stayin' out of it then?'

'Yeah, sure I am. Don't figure on ridin' no hundred miles or so just for the hell of it.'

Mitcham inclined his head, looked at him with his good eye.

'What you talkin' about?' he growled.

'Matthew Case. He quit town last night.'

Mitcham swore. 'When?'

'Smack on sundown. I reckon with him ridin' all night on that grey o' his, be could be a fair way across the Yuma Desert . . . if he went that way, that is. If he took the Casa Grande trail he'd be near the Gila Lakes.' Emple grinned mischievously. 'Of course, he could be buildin' himself a smoke on top o' Stand Up Rock. Then again, if he went — '

'Shut it, Emple. Shut your goddamn mouth.' Mitcham was infuriated, thrust his gun back into his holster. He touched his sore, split lips with the tips of his fingers, took off his hat and rubbed a hand through his hair. 'Which way *did* he go?'

'Now that I didn't see, friend.'

'You saw. You just ain't tellin'.'

Emple grinned widely at him. 'That's for me to know, Mitcham. But if you want some advice . . . go home . . . count your blessin's. Now, if you don't mind, I got another day to start, an' I don't want you clutterin' up my office . . . unless you figure on spendin' time in one o' these cells.'

Mitcham held the sheriff with a steely glare, then heeled about, stomped out on to the boardwalk. He looked thoughtfully up and down the street, made it along to Lome's stable. The boy remembered Matt Case all right, had taken a dollar off him. He confirmed that Case had taken his horse just after sundown the previous evening, had saddled it himself and ridden out.

Mitcham went back to his own horse and swung stiffly into the saddle. After giving Shave Emple another hard look as the lawman watched him from the jailhouse, he kicked his mount into a trot and rode from town.

10

Night Riders

Matthew Case forded Dog Creek for the first time, took a short rest and resumed his way. The Eagle Tail Mountains broke into long slopes where lush grassy meadows lay alternately with finger-shaped washes. An hour later, below the pine and spruce, he found the creek again, as Doc Pease had told him he would. He stopped, put his grey on picket in a small flat of grass and made a meal of two doughgod biscuits and creek water. A small, chill wind moved against him and he drew his blanket in, sat and watched the sun break.

At this hour the air was thin and clear, and when Matt rose the strike of his spur on a creekside rock rang a sharp echo along the edge of timber.

Shielding his eyes with his hat, Matt wondered if he was anywhere near where his father had once stood: wondered if it was the picture he'd had in mind when he'd said 'look to the country about, son'.

Twenty minutes later, using a short length of angle iron he'd picked up, Matt kicked away two aggressive geese while he levered open the back door of Homer Welles's house. He went into the low-ceilinged building and made a turn-your-stomach noise, reached for the first window and pushed it open. Then he opened all the windows in the other rooms, and the front door, noticed the old Hawken rifle in its rack above the lintel. He saw Homer's soiled work-clothes piled in a heap on the floor, an assortment of pans and plates stacked high and dirty on a table. There was a basin of murky water standing in a bowl, an iron pot that contained something that smelled bad. A side of bacon was hanging shiny and beginning to sour. None of it was that unusual:

just everyday chores that Homer would have eventually got round to taking care of.

Matt cut down the flitch, gathered the obviously unwanted rubbish and took it all out back. He got some dry leaves and sticks and made a fire of the waste heap. He watched it burn before going back to get the dead man's clothes, other flammable bits and pieces. In the scullery he pumped up some water, tipped away the foul, standing juices. Then he went across a small clearing to Homer's barn.

The barn was about in the same mess as the house and reeked of soiled straw and horse-piss. A few sacks of grain had been roughly split, the contents scattered along the fronts of the two horse-stalls. Two saddles hung on wall hooks but it looked like only one was usable. The spread had been running down and, like many old folk, Homer Welles had been chary of discarding anything that had some mileage left in it.

One of the horse corrals had a broken rail, another, fallen poles, but generally they were solid enough. Matt unsaddled his grey and turned it into the yard after fixing a low sapling bar, then he hefted his traps up into the barn loft. He worked for half an hour before he had a bagged straw mattress, his spartan belongings piled into an empty melon box. When he was satisfied that he'd got himself sorted, he saddled up an inquisitive cow pony that came to greet him and went to inspect the rest of the Welles property.

He got himself an impression of the land and its boundaries, made mental notes of the damaged fences, how the creek was silting up downstream. A long hour later back at the ranch house he took an early pull of his whiskey, contemplated the work ahead.

Matt figured it would take him five, maybe six days to get the house and its immediate surroundings fixed and tidied. After an unhurried smoke he took off his shirt and grabbed an axe he'd found in a lean-to tool-shed. He went on to the slopes and in the hot afternoon he swung at timber. It was a task which he knew about, was skilful at, and he had soon cut enough to make fence posts, and repair the barn and corrals.

That night he slept a weary sleep, and was up at first light. He started work on the north wall of the barn, remained until the noon heat drove him into the upstream creekwater. He rested for an hour and ate some more of his biscuit. This time though, he had them with wild onions and a goose egg. He found an unopened tin of condensed milk and some sugar and he made strong, sweet coffee. After his accustomed smoke, he started work again. Then at sundown, with his muscles jingling with the work of sawing and hammering, he stretched out on the porch to survey his labour. He watched the geese go for a lone heron that was probing the rushes for frogs. He was tired, but alert and more content than he'd been the night before.

He was sipping his whiskey from a tin mug when two riders came up from the creek. He sat in the dark shadows, only the intermittent glow from the tip of his cigarette marking his presence. He silently placed the mug at his feet and pinched out the tip of his smoke, sat unmoving.

The riders came on straight for the house. The geese hissed their alarm, but knew enough to stay away from the horses' hoofs.

'Old Homer liked his grog, we might get ourselves lucky this night,' one of the men said, as they pulled their horses up.

They were swinging from their saddles when Matt got up, walked slowly to stand in the doorway. Matt was light-footed, but his footfall made an ominous noise in the night silence. The two men stopped suddenly as they approached the porch steps, dropped hands to their side arms.

'Don't touch them guns,' Matt demanded, remembering that he'd wound his waistband around his Colt, left it in the melon box. He stretched an arm upwards, felt the breech of the Hawken above the door.

Alarmed and surprised, the men did as they were told. They gulped, looked hard at each other and backed off a pace.

'Who the hell's speakin', mister? This is Homer Welles's place,' the same man said. 'We're neighbours, an' we know *he* ain't here.'

'But you think his grog might be,' Matt said. 'An' luck ain't got nothin' to do with it. You were about to steal a dead man's bottle. Now, the two o' you move real slow while I get myself a little lamp goin' here. I wouldn't want to put a hole in either o' your bellies when I meant to take your legs out, now would I?'

'Who the hell are you?' the other man growled.

'I'm the hired hand,' Matt told him.

'Homer lived here alone. He never took on no hired hand.'

'I'm workin' for his niece,' Matt said flatly. 'You stayin' on for that drink?' he threatened.

The two men looked at each other again. In the shadow of the dark they could see Matt's raised arm, guessed where he had his hand. After a few moments thought, they backed towards their horses.

Matt remained very still, could just see them climb aboard their mounts.

'If you two ever come back, make sure it's daylight. I might just turn real unneighbourly. I got a real aversion to night riders.'

The man who'd spoken first sniffed and hawked.

'We'll be back, daylight or not,' he grunted. 'I'm goin' to get you checked out, mister.'

Matt drew back the hammer of the big-bored rifle, flinched as the deadly, metallic snap splintered the night.

'I've changed my mind,' he said. 'Get off this land, an' don't ever come back.'

The riders turned their horses. Matt

stood watching until he saw the break in the ribbon of light as they crossed the creek downstream. He thought they must have headed east, in the general direction of Coomer Spills's land. For some time Coomer Spills looked hard at his two hired hands.

'So, the old coot's got himself a niece, has he?' he asked.

'That's what he said, Mr Spills. Said that was who he was workin' for.'

'And who exactly was *he*?'

'Hired hand, he said. It weren't that friendly a meetin'.'

Spills frowned. 'Well, what did he look like?'

'It was dark, Mr Spills. You can't — '

'So you let him sweet-talk you? You never thought to bust him, just got your asses safely back here. Is that it?'

One of the two men showed surprise.

'Hell, Mr Spills,' he started. 'If you've ever heard the sound of a big rifle being cocked a few feet from your face, an' in the darkness, you don't stay around arguin'.'

Spills sighed wearily. In the last few days he'd realized just what a seedy and disorderly outfit he'd got on the payroll. He remembered it wasn't so long ago that he'd got good reliable men: rawhiders who knew their place, the way of things. But now he reckoned he was employing treacherous men who were getting the nod from Grod Mitcham rather than himself.

He looked up, in the light from his house lamps saw Niles Stockman and Mitcham walking towards him.

'These boys say there's a gun staked out on the Welles place, Grod. Do you know anythin' about it?'

Mitcham shook his head.

'Nope. I was in town most o' yesterday. Today I been workin' the bottom country with Clem and Niles.' He turned to the two men. 'A gun, you say? Who the hell was he?'

'They didn't see him 'cause o' the dark, an' they didn't get his name 'cause he didn't tell,' Spills mocked. 'All they did was ride away, come straight

125

back here.' Spills looked out at the two men, but he didn't know them well, didn't even know their names. He was wearying of that task, had mistakenly given Mitcham the responsibility of hiring new hands for the herding season. 'Tomorrow, we'll ride over and take a look at this feller,' he told Grod, firmly. 'It's no secret I want that land, so I suppose I'll have to go through the girl . . . Homer's niece, to get it. We'll leave at sun-up, might even go on into town if the deal means me seein' her personal.'

Spills then backed off, turned into the house. Mitcham looked up and followed, but the ranch owner was expecting it and closed his front door quickly. Mitcham pulled up short and his beaten face took on heavier colour. For a short moment, his eyes bored into the solid timber and he swallowed hard. Then he turned, stamped his way off the porch. He hurried across the yard followed closely by Niles Stockman.

'Looks like you just got the bullet

from Mr Spills's gang, Grod,' he said.

'Shut it,' Mitcham snarled. Before they went into the bunkhouse he turned sourly to Stockman. 'Tomorrow, you an' Clem get that section cleared out. Drive the cattle down the wash,' he said. 'I'll go with Spills, try an' keep him busy 'til we get them beeves on the run for Yuma. I want no mistakes, Niles. Anybody pokes their nose in . . . gets wind o' what's goin' on, tell 'em to see me. You're just carryin' out ramrod's orders.'

'We already got nigh on three hundred head, Grod,' Stockman contended.

'So? We want another hundred, maybe two if we can get 'em. I'm not pullin' out short if I can help it, an' Spills can afford it.'

Stockman said nothing more, watched the darkness close about Mitcham as he turned back towards the cookhouse.

Mitcham spent a quarter-hour tenderly bathing his face with brine water before he returned to the bunkhouse.

His whole body hurt, and his mind turned to a brown study: murderous thoughts. First, he was going to relieve his boss of four to five hundred head of good cattle. Then he'd drift, search out Matthew Case, probably kill him for the wounding.

11

Doubtful Agreement

Tilly Welles wasn't deterred from rising early. For two days she'd ventured no further than the outskirts of White Basin and Doc Pease had introduced her to many of the townspeople. So now, walking with the doctor to the livery stable, she began to take a different view of the town.

Her first reaction to it had been one of abject horror. From the window of the stagecoach, she'd seen no redeeming features, nothing that could possibly appeal to her. But now things seemed a little different. Those people she'd met who'd claimed friendship with her uncle, she found to be kindly and sympathetic to her predicament. She had even started to consider the town as a likely place for her to settle.

An eager nervousness gripped her as she climbed into the rig that Pease had hired to go and visit the Welles spread. Spending time with the doctor and Elspeth Barrow had given her something to think about. Now she owned something, could consider things other than the fripperies of the Prescott drapery.

It was a more optimistic Tilly Welles who drove out that morning with Harry Pease. As they waved to Elspeth, left the northern end of town, the sun burst through, lifted itself high across the distant Gila Lakes.

Pease waved an arm at the land ahead of them.

'I keep thinkin' o' Homer's place, but I guess it's yours now, Tilly. Yeah, it's your place that's set on those lush slopes, Dog Creek runnin' through it, an' plenty o' timber. Was a while back that I spent some time out there . . . doctor's rounds, you know. When that big sun hits the trees . . . ' Pease stopped for a moment, let the picture dawn. 'Oh yeah, it was pretty all right,' he continued thoughtfully. 'Makes me wonder why I spend so much time in town.'

'Because that's where the people are . . . the people who need looking after, I guess.' Tilly offered. 'It must be a good feeling for a man to have so many close friends . . . to have won their respect.'

'Hmmm. There's times when I think I'd rather have won somethin' else . . . an argument maybe. A seat on the State Legislature.'

'You're unhappy in White Basin?'

Pease shrugged, flicked the reins. 'Weary, bored to tears, more like it. An' that winnin' their respect ain't quite what it seems. I know of so many confidences, it's difficult for most o' them folk to be anythin' else, if you know what I'm sayin'.'

'What do you know about my uncle?' Tilly asked, before Pease got into maudlin.

'Hmmm,' Pease started uncertainly, 'You ain't goin' to like it girl. But then again it's only an accusation,' he came up with.

Tilly twisted in her seat to look at him, 'What accusation?' she asked.

Pease watched the track ahead of them as they took a long shallow bend. He let the horse settle into an even gait. He pulled one of his cigarillos, thought about it and put it back. Looking straight ahead he said:

'Homer was accused of being a rustler . . . a cattlethief.'

'Well, I do know what a rustler is, Doc. Who accused him of being one?'

'A neighbour o' his. Yours now.'

As if by instinct, Tilly's mind went back to her arrival in town, the fighting in the street.

'You can tell me, Doc,' she said. 'I'm not for swooning . . . not any more.'

'Grod Mitcham was one of 'em. They claimed Homer stole some of your neighbour's cattle . . . had 'em coralled on his land.'

'What neighbour?' Tilly asked curtly.

'Coomer Spills. Homer called 'em all

liars an' Mitcham set about him. That was when young Geronimo came along . . . stopped him being beaten up bad.'

'What Geronimo? What do you mean?'

Pease looked at Tilly's green-grey eyes. 'I mean Matthew Case,' he said. 'It's a tag that ain't funny, nowhere near accurate either. It's just that he's got some Indian blood in him.' The doc took a deep breath. 'An' I really have got to tell you about him . . . very soon,' he added, jiggled the reins again. 'Anyways, old Homer went for his gun. He was killed before he could do any damage with it, though. That was the shame of it. Even the sheriff agreed.'

The colour drained from Tilly's face and she bit her lip. She held her hands tight as Pease continued:

'The upshot was, your poor uncle lyin' dead in the street, an' Matt Case keeping the curs at bay until the sheriff arrived to jail him.'

'He was the man in the street wasn't he?' Tilly presumed.

'Yeah. He was the one standin'.'
Pease grinned, almost chuckled.

'And he was jailed for going to the
aid of my uncle. A old man who was
bullied and outnumbered?' Tilly asked.

'Yeah. Ironic, ain't it? But that ain't
the fault of Shave Emple, Tilly. He had
to do somethin'. It was Mitcham who
accused Case of bein' in cahoots with
Homer.'

Tilly screwed up her face. 'What?'
she said, dumbfounded. 'The sheriff
believed this? Didn't he know Homer?'

'It had nothin' to do with believin',
Tilly. But let me finish. I'd seen this
stranger ridin' into town earlier . . .
about an hour later than Homer came
by. I told this to Shave, wanted the boy
let out of jail. Of course he weren't in
cahoots with Homer. They'd never even
seen each other before.'

'How did he get out then . . . Matthew Case?'

'That's the curious thing. It was
Mitcham had his bail settled. I got to
give that some thought, Tilly. It don't

134

make much sense, not for what happened next.'

Tilly's concern showed, but for a while she thought deeply, kept her silence.

'Matt came down the street,' the doctor went on, 'and one of Mitcham's men drops a rope around his shoulders. He got dragged off the boardwalk, near pulled under the stage you were on.'

'Yes, I saw. I saw what happened next, as well.'

'Yeah, well, then Chawke came along. He was gunnin' for Matt. There was no other way.'

'And why doesn't that surprise me?' Tilly said scathingly.

'This ain't Prescott, Tilly. What Matt Case did enables him to fight another day. And that's what someone'll want him for.'

'Why?'

Pease stared into the distance as he answered, 'It's *him* that's out at the ranch. Your ranch.'

'I should have guessed. The good

doctor's got me a gunman to chop firewood and mend fences.'

'He's the man who sided with your uncle, Tilly. He could o' walked away . . . didn't know he had a choice. He's a good man.'

'Yes. I know. I'm sorry, Doc. I — '

'Forget it.'

'What did you mean when you said he'd be wanted for more fighting? More fighting on my land?'

'Out here Tilly, you got to be ready for most things. I guess gunfights are just the worst of 'em.' As he spoke, Pease drew rein and pointed ahead. 'Just down there,' he said. 'Along the slope and we cut the creek again, then it's your land, Tilly Welles. Why don't you sit quiet now . . . take it in . . . see if it ain't God's own country.' Pease smiled warmly. 'It's worth fightin' for. Homer knew it . . . wouldn't be pushed off.'

But Tilly couldn't see much of the country that stretched out before her. She was fighting it well, but her eyes were misted. From what the doctor had said, she was employing the man who'd shot someone dead in the middle of White Basin's main street. It was true that Matt Case had gone to the aid of her uncle. But if she stayed, she too would be involved in neighbour trouble, didn't know how to resolve the problem with the well-meaning doctor.

Pease worked the rig across the shallow bed of the creek crossing, sent it rolling easily up the long slope. Through the noises of harness and rig he heard the carried sound of a hammer smacking into clout nails. Then, of a sudden, the house was before them. The mid-morning sun touched the grass, beamed into the pine and spruce that edged the slopes around the compact building.

In spite of her troubled thoughts, Tilly couldn't hold back a short intake of breath when she saw the colour and richness of the land. It was pretty all right, shame to be spoiled by ugly brutes of cows, she thought.

137

'See? Pretty, ain't it?' Pease said.

Tilly nodded, let the house hold her gaze. She was afraid to look at anything else, lest Matt Case appeared as the mixed-blood Indian. The man who'd now reverted to the savage she'd created in her mind, with dime-novel tomahawk and war paint.

12

Neighbourly Encounter

'There's our man,' Pease said and pointed off to the left.

Tilly tried not to look but found her head coming about anyway. Matt Case was walking across the long eastern slope, the long haft of an axe in his right hand, his cambric shirt tied loosely around his waist.

Pease felt Tilly tighten up beside him. He reached across and gripped her arm.

'Ease up lass,' he said quietly. 'Might not be as bad as you think. Give out some slack, eh?'

But Tilly shrugged from his touch. 'No, I can't face him,' she said. 'I remember too well what happened. I saw his eyes. It's all come back. I didn't think it would.'

'I told you, he's a good man, Tilly. I know it,' Pease said defensively.

'How can you know that? He didn't carry recommendations on him did he?'

'This is still a frontier, Tilly. An' out here, there's other ways o' readin' a man. If you don't dig in, you'll get blown away. You said yourself you been somewhat sheltered. So, if you'll let me be blunt, ma'am, if you're aimin' to stay, it's maybe about time you looked at things as they actually are.'

'If you'll allow *me* to be blunt, Doc, it's that sort of opinion that's keeping White Basin a backwoods town, not a frontier one.'

Pease saw the firm set of Tilly's face, decided against continuing his homily.

Matt was close now, so he dropped the axe head to the ground and leaned on the haft. As the rig approached he looked up at Tilly, saw the rising mark of her awkwardness.

For Tilly Welles it was a curiously troubled moment. She was almost instantly moved by the contradiction of what she'd thought and what she saw.

'Hello, Matt. Miss Welles has come to look at the house . . . see what she thinks. You been workin' somethin' off, I see.'

'Yeah, a few aches an' pains,' Matt agreed, his eyes still on Tilly. 'But there's still a heap to do. Work that is.'

'Thank you for what you've done . . . what there's still to do . . . if you're interested,' Tilly found herself saying, albeit haltingly.

Matt nodded in response. 'I'll thank you for givin' me the chance to stay, ma'am. Not for the work, though, I aim to earn that,' he said.

Pease grinned indulgently. 'Yeah, you done good Matt. But now we got things to talk about.'

'It's goin' to get real hot under this sun. Why don't you get Miss Welles's luggage, take her into the house. It'll be cooler, an' away from them goddamn geese,' Matt said. 'I made me a nest in the barn, when you got time,' he added.

Pease noted Matt's candour, thought

he might have a double problem on his hands now. He climbed down from the rig, offered a hand to Tilly. Despite her obvious reluctance, he led her into the house. He could see she was uneasy, and there was stuff for her to see. He left her there looking at what were maybe family mementos, returned to catch up with Matt who was lifting a pail of water on to a table outside the barn.

'You don't need to get close to find out what temperature she's blowin', Doc. What exactly you been tellin' her about me?' Matt wanted to know.

'She's a draper's daughter from Prescott, Matt. Young an' impression-able too. Ain't looked too long into this world. Give her time.'

Matt shook his head. 'It's obvious she wants no part of this place, an' I reckon you knew it. But you want rid o' Grod Mitcham so much, you ain't goin' to see it. That's what I think.'

'Yeah, an' as if that weren't enough, she lost her pa a few months back.

There's no family o' hers left.'

Matt held up and stared confusedly at Pease. 'What the hell you tryin' to do then? I thought doctors were supposed to help.'

'I am, Matt. That's exactly what I'm doin' because somebody has to. I did tell her somethin' of what I knew about you on the way out here. But your escapades in town ain't exactly my fault, and nor is any opinion she's formed because of it. As for Grod Mitcham, you can cut an' run, that's up to you.'

Matt took a deep breath. With both hands he rinsed water over his face, rubbed at his chest and shoulders. But he was listening to Pease.

'If you stay, you'll have to accept each other, Matt. It's just goin' to take the girl a bit longer. For my part in it, well it's the thinkin'; there's just no stoppin' my mind workin'.'

'You better tell me then,' Matt said, sputtering water.

'It's no secret that Coomer Spills has

always wanted the tail section of this spread. Homer wasn't interested in sellin', though, not in part or the whole caboodle. So, acceptin' that Homer wasn't a cattle-thief ... which he wasn't, I reckon they killed him for it.'

Matt untied his shirt, asked, 'How would they've got it?'

'A land sale ... settlement o' property. There'd've been no claim, or opposition even. But like most of us, Spills never reckoned on a niece turnin' up.'

'Seems to me, you're sendin' us out along a cracked branch on that reckonin', Doc. What else you got on your mind?'

Pease was looking over Matt's shoulder, past the corner of the barn.

'Right now, those two riders,' he said, nodding out at the green pasture.

Matt turned and saw a rider who was obviously carrying some hog-high fat. He was sided by a grim-faced Grod Mitcham. Matt eyed them for a moment more, then stepped quickly into the barn. When he returned, he'd donned a long, skin shirt, held the Colt, which he placed on the table behind the water pail.

'You goin' to throw pills, or do you prefer that I handle this?' he asked the doc.

'I'm plumb out of ammo, kid. You're on your own,' Pease said with a friendly grin. 'But there don't have to be trouble, Matt. Let's move to the house, do our talkin' there. That's Coomer Spills ridin' with Mitcham. He knows better than to harm me. But for you, Matt . . . ?' Pease let the words hang before continuing: 'Well, for that, I'm sorry, I really am. But as I said, it really ain't my fault. Let me do the talkin', though. Maybe I can work my way round 'em.'

They set off across the yard and, under his breath, Matt swore his aggravation. Mitcham and Spills were well out of the timber now and approaching the back of the ranch house. Pease went on, but Matt stopped, held his ground. He stared hard at the two riders, saw the angry twitch of Mitcham's wounded jaw.

Spills gave a sharp signal with his right hand and Mitcham pulled his horse in behind him. Doc Pease stepped out from the front of the house and Tilly was alongside him. She looked straight at Matt, and her eyes blazed when she saw the gun he was holding down at his side.

Spills and his ramrod reined in, and the rancher removed his hat. He glanced speculatively at Matt before nodding at Tilly.

'Ma'am. I guess you'll be Homer Welles's niece,' he said.

Tilly nodded, didn't say anything.

Spills gave a fleeting smile. 'I'm Coomer Spills,' he said. 'I'm known to the doc here, an' vice versa, so we can get settled straightaways. Mine's the land that borders your lower slopes . . . the south boundary beyond the creek. It's regrettable what happened to your uncle, but — '

146

'Regrettable!' snapped Pease. 'What in the name o' God you talkin' about? You sent those sons o' bitches into town to gun down Homer. Four of 'em against one old man. Those always the sort of odds you go for, Spills?'

Matt saw the provocation in Spills's face, saw the muscles tighten. Mitcham shifted in his saddle, coolly weighed up Matt. Matt just leaned against the low veranda fence, placed his Colt on top of the handrail. He deftly built himself a cigarette, but his casual stance suggested a man who'd just as soon hold a gun in his hand. Coomer Spills saw it, if Mitcham didn't.

Spills shifted his horse a little closer to Pease.

'This is 'twixt me an' the girl. Butt out,' he snapped.

'That's where you're wrong, friend, You see, I'm advisin' *an'* prescribin' for Miss Welles. An' I will, until I'm advised otherwise.' Pease retorted. 'She don't know you, an' I'm rememberin' that Homer was a friend o' long standin'. So I ain't goin' to stand by an' let you cheat her out o' this ranch or anythin' else.'

Spills ground his teeth again. 'A thousand dollars ain't rightly cheatin'. That's the deal I had with Homer . . . the deal he accepted. Now I'm offerin' fifteen hundred.' Then Spills looked at Tilly, forced an arch smile. 'If you want to go on livin' here, that can be arranged,' he said. 'If you want to carry yourself with crops, play around with a horns-an'-bone herd, that too can be arranged. But you'll be working for *me*. Your adviser there'll tell you there's no percentage in bein' hasty. You can have until this evenin'. It's up to you.'

'I reckon you're wastin' your time, Spills. Yours, mine and hers. So why don't you take that bag o' buffalo guts an' go home.'

Spills thought for a moment. Then he backed up his horse a few paces and Mitcham came forward.

'Don't push your luck, old feller,' he

threatened, while taking a quick, sideways glance at Matt.

'Always have, son. Somethin' I learned at Chickamauga,' Pease told him. 'There was no other way. Just like now. An' talkin' o' those who push their luck, why don't *you* clear off this land. There's some of us got work to do.'

Matt flicked away his cigarette butt, flexed the fingers of his right hand. He was ready to move. Both Mitcham and Spills saw the slight movement, knew and recognized the intent.

'We takin' ultimatums from these two, boss? An old quack an' a 'breed drifter?' Mitcham questioned sourly. 'Why don't we teach 'em a lesson right here . . . deal with the girl after? She looks to me like a filly that don't like heat an' flies bothering her. Reckon she'd prefer town, with its comforts, like.'

Matt looked out at Spills, but kept Mitcham in his sight.

'If the lady wants you to stay, she'll invite you to get down. If not, she won't,' he said. He turned to Tilly and asked her. 'You want 'em to stay, ma'am?'

Tilly shook her head slowly. 'No, I don't,' she said. 'I want them please to leave my land.'

Matt tensed. He was set like a mountain lion and his eyes gleamed, bore deep into Spills's core.

'You heard,' he said, with frightful menace. 'The lady's given her orders. Now why don't you an' manure-mouth do as the doc suggests, an' ride off?'

Pease saw that Tilly had begun to tremble at the worry of Matt's obvious ultimatum. And his own pulse was racing as he took her arm gently.

'It's over, Spills. There's nothin' more to be said,' he called out as he guided Tilly back along the short veranda to safety.

But in the doorway she stopped,

'No,' she protested. 'I want to see what they do ... see what sort of neighbours they really are.' She looked beyond Mitcham to Spills, then she saw

Mitcham move. He kicked a heel into the belly of his horse, while at the same time grabbing for the revolver he wore high around his waist.

But he'd hardly cleared the leather of his holster before Matt had flashed his hand out to his own Colt atop the veranda handrail. In an instant, he had the blue-steel barrel pointing up into Mitcham's startled, overwhelmed face.

The blur of movement brought a gasp, then an oath from Spills. 'You're real adept with that gun, Mr Case. Not your everyday plough-chaser.'

'Yeah, I know. Must come as a real surprise. My pa once told me never to pull a gun unless I aimed to use it. He never told me about exceptions, though. I'll have to learn as I go along, I guess.' He smiled grimly at Mitcham, said with quiet venom. 'You want to risk it, you big, ugly son-of-a-bitch?'

Mitcham snorted loudly and shifted in his saddle. It was plain he was fighting down an urge to rush Matt. But it was a doomed challenge and his shoulders slumped. He sneered, lifted his hand away from his holster.

'There'll be another time, Case,' he muttered. 'You ain't finished with me.'

'Clear off,' Matt said. 'If there is a next time, I'll set the geese on you.' He crooked his arm and, against his thumb, opened and closed the forefinger of his right hand, hissed between his teeth in goosey derision.

Matt stood watching as the Spills pair moved off. It wasn't until they disappeared into the first stand of pine that he moved away from the house. Without another word from Tilly or Doc Pease, he'd heard the front door close. On his way to the barn his forehead was creased from his thoughts. He knew there was going to be trouble with Mitcham, but it didn't overly concern him. His bother was the opinion that Tilly Welles had formed of him. He was put out, because she'd seemed prepared for him to fight for her. Perhaps he'd have to reconsider his position. He wasn't the only one who could close a door on something he didn't like the look of.

He went into the barn, was muttering as he climbed the ladder to his lofty lair.

13

Early Days

Tilly Welles ran a finger along a shelf in the scullery, frowned at the dust deposits.

Watching her, Pease said, 'Homer weren't a tidy man, but he had honest values.' Tilly didn't say anything, so he went on. 'I'm sorry I took over out there, Tilly, but I know how Homer felt about this place. There's no way he ever meant to leave it . . . except to you. It's that what makes Spills a liar, an' I couldn't let him get away with it.'

Tilly walked thoughtfully from the small room. Not a window in the house had curtaining to keep out the harsh sunlight. The floor was solid puncheoned pine, but she doubted if it had ever been washed down, seen a broom even. The air, even for its recent airing, was stale, thick with the glow of rising dust motes.

'At least I can manage the cleaning, if nothing else,' she said, feeling the dirt clinging to her hair. 'It won't be done overnight, though.'

'Does that mean you'll stay?' Pease asked intently. 'That outburst o' mine wasn't in vain?'

'I might stay for a month. I had no real plan to sell before I looked the place over, you know, Doc. I didn't have anything before I came, so something's changed. Uncle Homer did write telling me how wonderful the country was. That means I wasn't going to sell up right off. Not before I gave the place, or me a chance. Even drapers' daughters from Prescott aren't that dim-witted.'

'Hmm, I guess not. What about Matt then?' Doc asked, uncertainly.

Tilly lifted the lid of a blanket box, fingered the contents with a glint of appeal.

'Homer didn't write me about him,'

she said, smiling. 'I really don't know. Giving it some thought is the least I can do, though.'

'Yeah, that's right, Tilly,' Pease responded. 'I can only imagine what first impression Matt gave you, but it was me asked him to came out here. In two days he's already got the place part fixed, if you overlook the dust. An' I don't think he's goin' off on a war dance over Mitcham an' Coomer Spills. I'd say he acted respectable-like, real committed.'

'Don't get too long on your praise,' Tilly suggested. 'He's got doubts.'

Pease laughed scornfully. 'Oh, yeah, he's got them all right. He knows how blood-spillin' affects you. No, Tilly. He acted just the way I thought he would. He's the man you're lookin' for right now.'

Tilly walked to the door, pushed it fully open. Pease came and stood beside her.

'Give it that month,' he said encouragingly. 'Whatever heaven on earth looks like, this'll be it, believe me. Coomer Spills wants to annex it so bad, that must tell you its true worth. You don't have to move, Tilly. You got a life right here. A good life.'

'I'd be happier if you knew more about Matthew Case,' she said.

'Well, he's got some rough edges, that's for sure. But you got to admit, he gets things movin'. Of course, if there's some other problem you got concernin' him, Tilly?'

'I'll be out here on my own. What do you think?' Tilly murmured.

Pease gulped, looked out towards the barn. 'I think it's about trust an' goodwill. Both hard to get, Tilly . . . but so easy to lose. If that's the sort o' thing that's worryin' you, you best ride out o' here right now. I'll take you back to town. You can sell up to Spills, take the coach right back to Prescott.'

'I'm sorry. Don't be annoyed. Doc. I got to adjust . . . need a little more time.'

'There ain't none, Tilly. If you want help, that is.'

Tilly was staring at the barn when Matt came out. She watched him lead his grey to the corral where he swung up and looked towards the creek. He had a coil of wire slung across his shoulder, a hammer, nails and staples in a saddle-bag.

'Give him a chance,' Pease said. 'Looks like he's givin' you one. I mean, how much do you need to know about hired help?'

For Tilly, the words carried their intended sting. But Pease was already down the steps, hurrying across the yard.

Matt saw him coming and waited. Pease removed his hat, dabbed at his forehead.

'I reckon I've won her round, Matt,' he said guardedly. 'She was worried you'd be wantin' more'n wages.'

Matt's eyes narrowed. 'What's changed her mind?'

'I hinted at Indians an' new moons an' bear grease . . . buffalo blankets.'

'You done me a favour, then?' he said drily.

Pease studied him for a moment,

breathed a big sigh. 'That's up to you. But it sounds like it's a chance she's prepared to take.' The doc gestured with his hands. 'Good luck,' he said. 'I know you'll do right by her. An' watch out for Grod Mitcham. As if it weren't enough, I noticed he had a gleam in his eye. Even if it was a touch bloodshot.'

He turned and walked away, but Matt called out: 'Hey, Doc. Hold up a minute.'

Pease looked back. 'Yeah?' he said uneasily.

'I don't know what you got in mind,' Matt said, 'but it might be best if you stayed away. Mitcham *will* make a play, an' when he does, I don't want you here. But after, well, I'll be movin' on. I ain't workin' for no woman.'

Pease gaped at him. 'Why in hell not? Her dollars're just as good as anyone else's.' Then he thought for a moment. 'Oh yeah, I forgot,' he said, and his face crumpled into a knowing grin. 'There's half o' you believes that womenfolk find

pleasure an' honour in humpin' firewood . . . doin' the chores. Well, suit
yourself, but I reckon you got to leave
that way of life on the Red River. An' I
don't mean no offence, son.'

'Well, there's some taken, Doc, an'
she's got to do the same . . . leave
behind them frilly bonnets,' Matt said.

'Yeah,' Pease said a little cheerlessly.
'Seems you both got a lot to leave
behind . . . a lot o' rethinkin' to do.' He
raised a farewell hand, and went back
to his rig. Clutching the reins he
watched Matt heel his grey off again,
down towards the creek. He swung the
rig around outside the front of the
house, called out to Tilly. 'You got
nothin' to worry about except maybe
worryin'. For the most part, leave him
be. He'll keep his own counsel most o'
the time. If you want me for anythin',
you know where to find me.' And with
that, Pease gave the horse its head back
to White Basin.

As soon as Matt was out of sight,
Tilly walked up to the barn. She saw

where he'd cleaned up, tidied sacks and sorted tack. The ladder to the loft had been fitted with a few new rungs and the north wall had been mended.

Looking up, she saw a shirt flapping in the breeze which came through a high window. She listened for a moment, then climbed up until she could see over the edge of the loft flooring. She saw his straw-bagged bedding, his few personal belongings in the melon box. On top was the Cree blanket band that Matt wore around his waist. Fascinated, she took another step upwards. She picked up one end of the sash, ran her thumb across the intricate, coloured-glass beads. She was shocked, couldn't believe that a seemingly brutal man could possibly own such an exquisite object.

Returning quickly to the yard, consternation lines appeared across the top of her pale, smooth face as she looked to where Matt had been riding. Then she went back to the house and opened one of her two bags. She changed into shirt and work pants, set to on the floorboards.

Matt rode into the yard at sundown. He was tired, encrusted with dried sweat and dust, but he looked quietly satisfied. From a front window where she'd been sitting for some time, Tilly saw him pull off his shirt, wash himself down from the water pail outside the barn. In the yellow sunset, and for a moment, she was curiously moved by the stick of his wet glossy hair to the muscles of his neck. But then she sniffed and turned away, went to fix up a cold supper. There was chicken, pickled eggs, cheese and a large slice of peach pie, starter foodstuff that Elspeth Barrow had thoughtfully packed into the rig.

As darkness began to settle Tilly lit up an oil-lamp and a string of happy jacks. Instinctively, she started to set out a table, but thought better of it. Instead, she set Matt's meal on a trencher and carried it to the door.

Matt was standing in the doorway of

the barn, smoking. When he saw her he tossed the cigarette aside and went forward to meet her.

'I'll bring the plates back in the mornin'. Thank you, an' good-night, ma'am,' he said quietly, accepting the tray.

Tilly brushed a long strand of dusty hair from her face, realized she'd not bothered to tidy herself since noon. She was still wearing work clothes she'd last worn when sweeping the stoop of her father's store in Prescott. As Matt looked at her, she hoped the fading light would disguise the rising colour in her cheeks.

'Thank you, ma'am,' Matt said again. 'That's real thoughtful. Tomorrow I'll be gone early. The creek needs to be dragged off where it's siltin'. If you want me for anythin', thump a stick against somethin'. I'll hear it an' come runnin'.' He smiled, then was gone and Tilly returned to the house. She sat down and looked at the wedge of cheese, the sliver of pie she'd left herself. As the tears welled in her eyes she brushed her hand angrily at a fat blowfly. She started to tremble, felt the crush of isolation and loneliness.

14

First Call

Tilly heard Matt ride off in the morning, was woken by the sound of the grey's hoofbeats. She was surprised to find the light was already creeping around the edges of a blanket she'd pressed into the window surround. Dressing hurriedly, she went to the scullery and found that he'd already replaced his two supper plates. Somehow, she knew they'd be there, but was shocked at discovering that Matt had entered the house while she slept. She moved to the front door, saw him riding down the grass-covered slope, only his head and shoulders visible above the early, low-curling mist.

Tilly's shoulders drooped. She didn't know how to take Matt . . . what to make of him. She went back to the scullery, ate the food she'd left untouched the night before. She saw the chopped timber that he'd piled against the wall inside the back door, the freshly pumped water in a big pitcher on the table. It was helpful, kind even, but didn't do much to allay the fear that he'd invaded her privacy.

It also highlighted just how much work lay ahead. Although Tilly worked hard all morning, scrubbing, tidying, moving stuff around, she still didn't seem to be achieving much. Eventually she lifted down the scattergun from above the door. She ran the back of her hand along the twin barrels, felt hard smoothness as she gripped the stock. Then she made window curtains from the dress she'd travelled in. She thought maybe the main room started to look like someone's home, if not yet hers. It saddened her to think of her uncle not having much in the way of comforts, but this time she stopped short of a snuffle.

Matt returned at noon. He hitched

the grey in the overhanging lee of the barn, flipped his hat over the pommel of his saddle. He washed his face and walked to the house. Outside the front door he called out, waited a moment for Tilly to appear in the doorway.

'I let myself in earlier . . . had an egg. I didn't disturb you, did I? I got my own coffee-makin's in the barn.'

'No, that's all right. I never heard a thing,' she heard herself saying.

'I got to thinkin', though. If you want, you can lay out some jerky for me. Perhaps some bread . . . drippin's, maybe, when you get set up. I can eat in the saddle.'

'That sounds dreadful . . . doesn't sound like it would keep a mouse alive,' Tilly said quickly. 'I thought all cowboys ate hugely.'

'I ain't really a cowboy, ma'am. I was brought up on mudfish, nuts an' snake. What I'm askin' you for's a real treat.'

Tilly looked askance at Matt for a moment, raised her chin and half-smiled. 'I do have a lot to learn, I know,' she said. 'Don't worry, I'll make sure you get well fed.'

'I got to make a pen for them godda . . . Sorry ma'am, them *geese*, before they peck my legs to pieces.'

'Yes, a good idea. Will you always have to work this long?' Tilly asked.

'As long as I'm here, ma'am . . . yes,' Matt said slowly, trying to measure the implication. 'I don't want to burn up in the heat of the day. So for the time bein' I'll be goin' out an hour before sun-up. I'll come back at eleven. After a bite, I'll work until the sun starts to drop . . . around four.'

'There's that much to do, is there?'

'Well, I sure ain't makin' it up. The fences come first, I reckon. Most of 'em need tendin', an' they won't wait.'

'Yes,' Tilly said quietly.

Matt nodded, turned and walked away.

'The pump doesn't work properly,' she called after him. The words came tumbling, and she realized she must have sounded anxious, as if she wasn't keen to see him go. She took a breath. 'At the side of the house,' she added. 'There's no draw from the pump. Could it be the well's run dry?'

'No ma'am. Not on this slope. One o' the good things about the place. I'll take a look at it.'

'Thank you. I'll prepare some food. Will you want to eat it here?'

Matt smiled, pointed to the back of the house. 'I'll be workin' out there this afternoon. There's some fruit trees need cuttin' back an' there's a feeder ditch needs clearing out. Doc Pease said there's a market in town every week. Come the fall, you could make some money sellin' apples.'

Tilly smiled in return, watched Matt go to the trough above which the pump was set up. Then she went straight back to the house and plumped herself into a chair, knew she should have controlled her emotions better. Matt Case was the hired help; a man with whom she could never have anything in common. But as soon as she'd thought it, Tilly recognized just how wrong she was.

Matt dismantled the pump and found the seals were worn away. Then he went to the barn and cut leather from the skirt of one useless saddle to make two new ones. Half an hour later when Tilly came out with his food she saw the trough filled to overflowing.

'What was wrong?' she asked.

'Nothin' much. It just needed fixin',' he said, and thanked her for the trencher.

Again, Tilly was perplexed, felt a curious frustration in the way they conversed.

Matt tugged at the brim of his hat, went to settle in the shade of a fruit-tree circle which Tilly's uncle had planted. He was mopping at gravy, contemplating a smoke, when he saw Tilly come around the corner of the house with two mugs of coffee. She was only twenty feet from him; he was still thinking about what to say, when a bullet spat into the ground between them. It was almost instantly followed by the echoed crack of the rifle that fired it.

Tilly stopped walking, her mouth opened and closed and she dropped the coffee mugs. She made a small, choking cry, looked stunned at Matt then started to tremble.

Matt got to his feet and turned in one smooth movement. Tilly saw him swing up the gun that he'd obviously had at his side as he sat eating. She lifted her hands to her face, took a step backwards. Then a second bullet smashed into the wooden platter, sent Matt's food plate and his fork flying into the air.

Matt swore. Then he yelled at her. 'Get to the house. Go now!'

Tilly stood there shaking her head, swaying unsteadily. She saw Matt holding out one hand towards her, pointing his gun at the timber where everything appeared normal, unmoving.

'For God's sake move, woman, or

we'll both die out here,' he screamed at her, his eyes bright with anger.

The noise of Matt's threat shocked Tilly from her frozen fear. She turned suddenly and fled for safety.

As soon as she rounded the corner of the house, Matt started to make his way through the trees. Running from the orchard and up the grassy slope, he saw Niles Stockman and another rider bearing down on him from the timber stands. He swerved to the left, and ran for a big, fallen spruce. He vaulted the tree and rolled down into its dirt-filled depression. Then he quickly regained his footing, levelled his gun hand across the broad tree-trunk and opened fire.

Three of Matt's quick-fire bullets ripped across the heads of the men's horses, causing them to buck and rear. The riders were trying desperately to gain control, bring their own guns to bear on him as Matt ran from cover.

Stockman saw him coming up fast and wheeled his terrified cow pony about. He cut it into a run and rode the top of the slope. His companion, slower to move, saw Matt too, and after firing off a shot whipped his horse the other way.

Matt scrambled up the slope, weaved around some felled perimeter trees. He saw Stockman riding into a long, narrow wash, while the other rider was already moving through boot-high grass on the other side. He pushed his gun into his pants top and carefully wiped the sweat and root dirt from his hands, waited for the two men to ride from sight.

He was in no doubt that the attack on him and Tilly had been carelessly planned, and it confused and worried him. Matt was sure Mitcham would have come after him himself, would probably have brought more backing than Stockman and another cowhand.

Matt pulled his gun and ejected the spent cartridges, refilled the cylinder from a handful of bullets he kept in his pocket. Then he turned and made his way back to the fruit grove. He was approaching the back of the house when he saw a rider coming fast along the wagon road. He broke into another run, faster this time, when he recognized the red, meaty face of Grod Mitcham.

Mitcham saw Matt, too, and wheeled his horse off the track. He rode straight at Matt, his vengeful eyes blazing. But Matt had outguessed him in time, made a desperate headlong dash for the cover of the water trough along the side wall of the house.

Mitcham had drawn his gun, fired fast and indiscriminate. His bullets cracked into the trough, whined off the pump head that Matt had just repaired.

Matt swore as he hit the ground. He rolled, raised himself on his elbows and loosed off two shots in return. Wet dirt spat up into his face and he lay down again, rubbed at his eyes with the sleeve of his shirt.

'I'm gettin' real sick an' tired o' you, Mitcham,' he then yelled, getting to his feet. He stood with his back to the wall

174

and brought up his Colt. Just before Mitcham swung his horse's head away, Matt fired.

It was a calculated shot, the only one he had time to make and it missed. Bent low in the saddle, the Spills foreman was away. Matt stretched out his arms, watched the man ride away through the gun's sights. He couldn't pull the trigger for fear of hitting the horse, and he'd never do that. Matt walked towards the fleeing figure, fired one ill-omened shot into the air.

When Mitcham was out of range, he stopped at the edge of the timber. He looked back for a moment, then, lashing down at his horse's gleaming shoulders, he raced away.

Matt plunged his head into the trough, shuddered and gulped in the fresh, cool water. Then he rubbed his hands up his face into his hair. As he walked to the front of the house he took the remaining bullets from his pocket, gripped them in his fist.

'One o' these is for you, Mitcham,

you son-of-a-bitch,' he said breathlessly.

There was deep silence now. Even the geese had found sanctuary under the floor timbers of the house. From near the front door Matt called out:

'Miss Welles.'

With no immediate answer he called again, 'Miss Welles . . . ma'am,' tentatively added, 'Tilly.' then waited a long minute before he heard her telling him to go away.

'OK, if that's what you want,' he said, relieved that she wasn't hurt. 'An' don't go worryin' about them visitors. It's over now.' He was still unsure, but after a few seconds more he added, 'They won't be comin' back.' Then he turned and walked across to the barn. Five minutes later he had on his black coat, wore his beaded band around his waist. He led his horse out into the yard, climbed slowly into the saddle.

From a front window Tilly watched him nervously. All she could think of was the harsh words he'd yelled at her. But somehow there was a difference now, and she felt a pang of shame. It was for her, on her land, that he'd stood resolute, faced the bullets fired point blank at him.

She saw him ride from the yard, away beyond the barn. She went quickly to the door, lifted out the security rail. She stepped out on to the veranda and waved her hand.

'Mr Case. I'm sorry. I am all right,' she called, listened to the empty, echo of her words.

15

Invitation to Ride

Matt rode down to the creek and made straight for the Spills ranchlands. In the past two days he'd traversed a sizeable section of the Welles place, had discovered that Homer's fencing abutted not only fertile Spills land but vast tracts of desolate scrub. He cut through a section of fence and, with his hat pulled down hard over his eyes, headed west across the Spills wasteland. He saw ground-covering plants which were tickseed and mallow, better understood the gain in old Homer's access to fresh, sweet water.

As he rode, his mind kept going back to the attack on the ranch, to Tilly Welles. He wondered, worried that he should have remained, just in case the Spills men returned. But after a while, a

178

slight, dawning smile broke across his face. Yeah, that was it, he thought. Exactly what he was supposed to think. Mitcham carried a rifle, could've dropped him from a distance if he'd wanted to. The attack wasn't as carelessly planned as Matt thought it was. It was a foray to draw fire, a ploy to keep him off the range.

He was riding along a low, stony ridge that rose into higher country, when he sighted the dust. It was a way off, to the south, and he reined in to watch. But it rose above a long finger of pine that ran down from the main timber. He headed off deeper into Spills country, pushed the grey for a few more miles until the land evened out.

The land was set out on big, gentle rising slopes, and of a sudden he could see the dust again, closer and more clearly. He saw the slow-moving, patchy carpet, the bobbing brown heads of the longhorns. It looked like four riders driving the herd, but the trail dust was thick and he was still too far away to be sure. He sat awhile and watched the advance of the herd, wondered why Spills was moving cattle through the crushing heat of the day.

Matt eventually drew back, rode to the other side of the ridge. He swung down into a shallow valley, followed a fence until it came to a run of the creek. He crossed in the shallows, let the grey slurp some water before taking a run at the far slope. Within minutes he was looking down into another long trough of country, only this time it was well grassed, had a collection of buildings spread midway along its northern aspect.

'Coomer Spills,' Matt said aloud. 'That's just got to be you.'

He found a scrub pine and climbed from his horse. With his back against the bole of the tree he hunkered down, built himself a smoke. From the ranch, he'd be silhouetted against the skyline, would have been an easy see for a look-out. He expected somebody to ride out to meet him with a rifle, but no one came.

Twenty minutes later Matt was closer than a quarter-mile from the sandy yard that fronted the main ranch house. Only then did he notice movement from along the columned terrace of the two-storey building. The rest of the vast spread appeared to be deserted. He walked the grey steadily beneath a timbered archway, picked out the lone figure who was standing deep within the shade of the house's upper balcony.

When he was thirty yards from the porch rail, Coomer Spills stepped forward and levelled a big Spencer rifle on him. But coolly, Matt held the rancher's concentration while he allowed the grey to keep going.

Spills moved a step sideways to position himself alongside one of the columns.

'That's far enough, mister, you ain't been invited in,' he rasped.

Matt let his horse walk a few more paces into the slanting shade before he drew rein.

'You need some iron to ride in here,' Spills said.

'Why? I ain't done wrong by you, have I?'

'Mitcham don't think like that. He could be here, just bustin' to strip your hide,' Spills suggested.

'I don't think so, Mr Spills. Anyways, I rode down here to talk to *you* . . . to ask you somethin',' Matt said.

'Ha. You decided to light out? You an' that interferin' Pease goin' to let the girl sell up as she pleases?'

Matt shook his head. 'No. No such luck.'

'What is it then? What do you want?'

'Well, I'm learnin' Mr Spills. So I'm curious to know why a smart rancher would herd cattle in this heat?'

Spills regarded him suspiciously. 'What the hell you talkin' about? What cattle . . . where?' he asked.

'Back aways. They're bein' pushed through that badland o' yours. I never got close enough to check the brand, but they certainly ain't Welles stock.'

'A herd?' Spills asked incredulously.

'Yeah, an' runnin' fast enough to lose most o' their lard. Must be pushin' three hundred head. That's a herd, ain't it?' Matt looked around him, then asked, 'It's sure quiet here. Your men out takin' a picnic . . . a potlatch in the badlands?'

'What's that got to do with you? You come ridin' out here to cause trouble, Case?'

Matt shook his head. 'No, why would I do that? Havin' you for a neighbour don't concern me much either way. But just a couple of hours back, Mitcham an' Stockman an' another o' your rabble paid the Welles place a visit. Mitcham fired off some shots . . . came real close to nailin' me. Now *that* concerns me, Spills. But you know, I got to thinkin' afterwards. What they was really tryin' to do, was make me stick real close to the ranch house. Close to Miss Welles's skirts, if you get my meanin'?'

Spills was plainly confused. He took

a step towards the porch steps, held the rifle barrel across the terrace railings.

'What the hell are you gnawin' at, Case?'

'As far as I know about this country, there's no other ranches this side o' Dog Creek. So those men I saw could be — probably *are* — your hands . . . drivin' your cattle. That's what they never wanted me to see.'

Spills's mouth twisted into a sneer.

'My men are checkin' the fences, cleanin' out Copper's tank ready for next month's drive. That's what they're doin'.'

'No, they ain't. Come take a ride, we'll see who's right,' Matt suggested.

'Go to hell.'

'I may well be. But you're comin' with me, Spills. I got a claim in this trouble.'

'You got a claim? What the hell's it got to do with you anyway, whether my cattle are bein' herded or not?' Spills demanded.

'I think it was old Homer Welles

tellin' me that he never stole cattle . . . never. But the truth didn't stop one o' your men shootin' him dead. That's one reason.' Matt's voice hardened as he continued. 'Then, o' course, there's your ramrod. I ain't goin' to sleep too well at night, just knowin' he's out there somewhere. Maybe he got himself a case o' buck fever today, so I'd like to give him another chance. Stockman can buy in, an' maybe a couple o' the others, if they feel that loyal to him.'

'You think you're that good, cowboy?'

After a fast, almost imperceptible movement of his right hand, Matt was holding his Colt, the barrel pointed straight at Spills's broad chest.

'I think maybe I'm good enough,' he advised with a thin smile. Right now, if you pull the trigger o' that Spencer, we'll both die. So you got to ask yourself, is it worth it, Spills? Lookin' around, you got a hell of a lot more to lose than me.'

Spills didn't appear to be bothered by Matt's take on the situation, although he dropped the rifle barrel.

'These men?' he asked. 'Which way they headed?'

'West. An' the longer we stand here powwowin' the further we'll have to ride. If we lose the sun it won't be any easier travellin' in that country . . . even for a Cree 'breed.'

Spills's breathing was heavy as he growled: 'I'll get me a horse. By hell, Case, we'll have ourselves a powder-burnin' contest if you're wrong.'

Matt nodded. 'You should be concernin' yourself with what'll happen if I'm right.' he said, calmly pushing his gun back into his waistband.

16

Night into Day

A short while later Matt turned his horse from the yard and Spills followed. Together they rode off the home pastures and headed west.

Matt took the lead, for two hours worked his way into the bare country. The deep-red light of the setting sun was slanting into their eyes when they first found the lifeless, crushed ground of the drive.

'What the hell's goin' on?' Spills said. 'There ain't no cattle on this side of the range other than Welles's stock, an' them blackjacks couldn't make it across Dog Creek, let alone to Yuma.'

'You want we should go back?' Matt asked.

'Hell, no,' Spills barked and heeled his horse forward.

They travelled another ten miles before Matt pointed ahead. The herd was settled, heads down around a cluster of hog wallows. Five men were riding close, giving the cattle a lick of water before taking advantage of the rustler's moon, pushing on through the night.

Spills dragged his big rifle from its scabbard, but Matt sided his grey with the other horse.

'We don't know who we're shootin' at,' he said. 'Best wait for mornin'. The risin' sun'll give us the edge we need. Meantime you can decide what you're goin' to do.'

'What *I'm* goin' to do?' Spills questioned.

'Yeah. I figure they're your cattle.' Matt swung down from his horse. He stretched out on the warm ground, pulled his hat over his eyes.

Spills slapped the barrel of his big rifle against his leg.

'You figure to sleep, with them owlhoots makin' off with the herd?' he

asked irritatedly.

'*Your* herd!' Matt snapped back. 'An' I'll hear 'em when they move out, which won't be long. For the minute, I ain't goin' nowhere. I've been doin' work I ain't rightly used to . . . got aches in muscles I never knew I had.'

Spills got down from his horse, let it mouth a tuft of cheatgrass.

'What work's that, Case?' he wanted to know.

'Fixin' up the Welles place. She's goin' to stay, you know . . . Miss Tilly. She's like one o' them Red River boats . . . got an oak keel, probably some of her uncle's stubborness, too.' Matt lifted his hat away from his face, looked up at Spills. 'What *was* your bellyache with old Homer? Musta been somethin' besides creek water?'

Spills thought for a moment before he answered.

'As with most things, he left his fences to rot. His longhorns strayed on to my place an' mixed with my Herefords. He should've been more careful . . . should've moved on, but instead he *hung* on, stubborn as a mule.'

'And that's why you branded him a cattle-thief? Sent four o' your men into town to beat up on him . . . kill him?'

'No, I never did that,' Spills railed, not liking Matt's charge. 'I've never sent anyone to do my work, Case. Not that sort o' work. It weren't so long ago that I fought to keep every goddamn blade o' grass. There was hardly a man for hire you could trust, an' I saw off nesters an' sheepmen. I had to drive cattle right the way to Mexico to get me a fair deal. No mister, I never needed to send men to do my work.'

Matt kept quiet. Without saying so, it was the nearest he could get to letting Spills know he believed him.

Spills stared out to where the herd was still watering. He rubbed the grey stubble of his chin, kicked each foot as if trying to move trapped grit around.

'Looks like they're gettin' ready to move 'em out.' he said.

He went to his horse and Matt did the same. For the next few hours they rode beyond the herd's dust, pushing further west across the hostile, darkening country.

★   ★   ★

'Hold up,' Matt called. He rode his horse across the front of Spills, and the rancher drew rein.

'What is it?' Spills asked.

'There's Copa Gully up ahead. If we ride the higher ground we'll be lookin' down on 'em. Should be close enough for you to let me know if they're your riders.'

Already the early light was good enough for Spills to see a mile ahead. But a thick cloud of yellow dust hung as a screen between him and the slow-moving herd. A westerly breeze whipped that dust back at him, forced him to ride with a neck cloth pulled high around his face.

He could see that Matt was working

his way up a long sloping trail, reluctantly decided to follow him. They rode steadily higher for close to another hour, and then, with the sun beginning its long, daytime burn, they reached a plateau that flattened off beyond the gully.

Matt was stopped there and he climbed from the saddle.

'We've got ahead of 'em,' he said. 'They got to come through here, but they won't see us. We'll wait up.'

Spills compassed the country about him, then he hitched his horse back out of sight. He brought the Spencer, and flattened himself on the ground beside Matt.

'I'm hopin' you ain't right about Mitcham,' he said. 'But by hell, if you are, I want the treacherous dog all for myself. You hear me, Case? He's mine.'

Matt shrugged. 'Mitcham's goin' to make the play. An' when he does, I won't be waitin' for you to take over. Sorry, Spills.'

Spills studied him grimly for a

moment but said nothing. Below them, the lead cattle were already moving into the head of the gully with the remainder of the herd in straggled lines behind. The five riders were bunched close, as if their lives were to be saved that way. Matt lifted a hand, shaded his eyes for a while.

'Can you make 'em out yet?' he asked.

'Can hardly see a goddamn thing,' Spills complained.

'Yeah. We'll see better when they're below us . . . won't be lookin' into the light,' Matt said.

They waited while the hot sun got higher, powered down on to their backs. There was a breeze that drifted up into their faces, but it carried hot, peppery dust from the desert floor.

Slowly the herd came on, and Spills continually rebuked one and all as he waited for the riders to move up close enough for naming. When the untidy spread began to bunch up directly below them, Spills raised himself to get a better view. Matt knew that anybody looking up couldn't see them against the high sun and kneeled alongside him.

Spills hissed a curse as he pointed down to the first rider.

'Stockman. Niles Stockman,' he growled. 'An' Clem Rollo, damn his hide. Never did like the look of him . . . eyes set too close together.'

Matt was smiling to himself as Spills jumped to his feet. The rancher hurried for his horse, was in the saddle before Matt had fully considered the situation. Matt shook his head, walked to his grey and coolly gave chase. He wasn't overly concerned, even relieved that Spills took the trail that would bring him out at the head of the herd.

Spills had drawn fifty yards clear by the time Matt reached the bottom of the sloping trail. When Spills sensed he was being caught, he slowed his horse to a trot.

'This is my fight,' he shouted.

'They're my cattle, my men and they're on my land.'

Matt drew alongside the fierce rancher.

'I don't care a goddamn spit in hell about any o' that, Spills. But no one's firin' a gun at me when they've a mind, you hear?'

Spills cursed, swallowed his reckless attack. 'OK, we let the herd go by,' he snapped out. 'But then I'm goin' for 'em. You got that, Case?'

Even as they spoke, Matt was working his way across the gully. The lead steers trod wearily between them, tossed their heads uneasily and continued. The bulk of the herd then crowded mindlessly past in their wake.

Shielded by an outcrop, Matt sat his horse. Across from him Spills, too, sat hunched forward in the saddle. He was seething with fury, peering into the low pall of dust and trying to stifle a thick cough.

Matt was looking for the last of the herd, saw Spills kick his horse away from the gully wall. As the dust thinned he saw him riding straight for the drovers. The Spills men were all riding drag, picking up stragglers, when through the rolling carpet of dirt they saw their boss, Coomer Spills, bearing down on them.

17

Against the Sun

Niles Stockman shouted a warning. He wheeled his horse about, and the others drew rein, stared ahead, unbelieving.

'Yeah, it's me, the one who pays you . . . you thievin' scum. Prepare yourselves,' Coomer Spills yelled. He pulled a big Colt from his holster and took the centre ground, threw shots ahead of him as he raced forward.

The riders broke apart, and Stockman swerved for a wall of the gully. He saw Matt Case coming towards him and fired. The gun roared in the steep rocky confines, the bullet slicing across Matt's left arm.

Matt issued a comforting word to his grey, moved the horse's flanks in close to the walls of the gully. He gritted his teeth, brought his Colt to bear on

Stockman. The injury to his arm was bloody but slight. He recalled his father's words about being caught in a gunfight.

You've maybe learned about one trusty bullet bein' enough if right's on your side? Well, forget it son. Go for the belly, an' put in three.

Two of Matt's bullets hit Stockman. One of them smashed into the man's side as he tried to swing his horse away. The other hit him below his ear, as he jerked forward in the saddle.

As its rider took the bullets, Stockman's horse whirled about, threw up its forelegs in an attempt to scale the gully walls. Then it slammed its hoofs back into the ground, and Stockman was pitched from the saddle. His body spread-eagled into the gully floor, where the dirt immediately crusted the broken flesh of his face. His horse squealed its terror and took wild flight.

Spills saw the shooting and cursed violently, looked about as Clem Rollo's bullet thumped into his upper leg. He groaned with the searing stab of pain, but was a wronged man and galvanized with hardiness and rage.

As Rollo thundered towards him, he reined in and threw his handgun to the ground, pulled the Spencer rifle. He lifted the big gun over the shoulder of his horse and fired at point-blank range at the cowhand.

'Meet your maker, boy,' he rasped.

Rollo threw up his arms as the flat-nosed .52 bullet exploded into his chest. He went backwards then sideways with one foot remaining trapped in its stirrup. Like Stockman his horse veered away in panic, headed back towards the end of the gully. Matt was holding his arm, watched in heart-thumping disgust as the horse sped by, Rollo's lifeless body rolling and twisting a thin trail of bloodied dust.

Matt swallowed hard. He patted his grey's neck, looked back to where the drover had ridden from. He saw the other three riders had withdrawn, were sitting their horses with their hands spread and away from their holstered guns.

He rode slowly down the gully to confront them. His eyes were wary, and he rested his gun hand across the horn of his saddle. Just ahead of him, Spills was moving too. The rancher was hurt, but cautious and astonished too, because he'd come close to being killed by his own men.

'Don't know what in tarnation's goin' on here, Mr Spills, but we been takin' orders,' one of the drovers spoke up hastily.

'Takin' orders from who?' Spills demanded.

'Grod Mitcham. He said to get the herd on to the barrens . . . through Copa Gully,' the man said anxiously. 'We didn't figure it was right, Mr Spills. Me nor the boys here, an' that's the truth.'

'It's a goddamn duck to keep me from stringin' you up,' Spills rasped. 'What's your name, mister?'

'Brendan Lemmer,' the man said.

'We was hired by Mitcham a week ago.'

Spills had a severe look at the two other men.

'Mitcham told us there was work if we wanted it. Never planned to rob the big house,' Lemmer said.

Spills glowered at him. 'Some likely damn yarn,' he said.

'Ain't no yarn, Mr Spills. It was like Bren told you. We never took from no one,' said another man.

'I'll remember you said that, Mister,' Spills threatened.

'You can check our guns, they're cold. Anyhow, they'd probably blow up in our faces if we used 'em,' the man offered as a further defence.

Matt reached out his hand, took the gun from Lemmer. It resembled Matt's own Colt, but was a cheap imitation of the real thing, made a harsh grating noise when he spun the cylinder.

'Leave 'em be, Spills,' he said. 'It's Mitcham we both want.'

Thompson, another of the drovers, pointed back along the trail.

'He pulled back, mid-afternoon. Said he was goin' to check with Mr Spills about pushin' the herd through the night. He should've been back by now.'

Matt worked his horse closer, looked at the doubtful Spills. 'We're wastin' time. Their story sits well with me,' he said.

Lemmer tipped the brim of his hat, nodded obligingly. Then he looked straight at Spills.

'Them cattle o' yours'll be runnin' off good fat,' he said. 'We best get after 'em . . . turn 'em back to pasture. What do you say, Mr Spills?'

Spills rubbed a gnarled hand across his face, looked back through the gully.

'What about Stockman an' Rollo? You goin' to take care o' them too?' he growled.

'If we don't, them buzzards will,' Lemmer said, inclining his head to the clear blue sky.

A malevolent grin crossed Spills's face. 'Yeah,' he muttered. 'They're circlin' on an ill wind, sure enough.'

'I'm interested in where you made the pick-up,' Matt said to Lemmer.

'They were corralled on land beyond the creek. They been there for a couple o' days,' Lemmer told him.

'Welles country,' Matt confirmed. He recalled he'd not ridden that far, knew that for the sake of a few more miles and Mitcham's strike at the ranch, he'd have stumbled on the herd, known that trouble was in the wind.

'My cattle on Welles country,' Spills said quietly, as if to himself.

'They're still runnin', Mr Spills,' Lemmer went on. He'd slowly lowered his hands, was twitching his reins.

Spills thought for a moment, looked hard at the riders.

'OK, go get 'em,' he ordered. 'We'll talk everythin' out later.'

Lemmer and the other two turned their mounts and rode off. Matt sat his horse, flexed his fingers as the sting in his arm spread to his hand.

'You been elected? 'Cause you're sure losin' a mess o' blood,' he said, seeing the dark wet spread down Spills's leg.

'I been nominated. But I'll live.'

'Looks like Homer didn't die for nothin',' Matt said tellingly.

'Looks like it,' Spills accepted. 'One day maybe I'll get to thank him. In the meantime, I'll just burn me a deeper brand into Mitcham's hide.'

'Maybe Tilly Welles would like to hear somethin' from you,' Matt suggested.

'Don't get me wrong, Case, I ain't rollin' over. That land business ain't finished yet. I'm still aimin' to get the girl to sell up. What's more, I ain't payin' you no respects for today's work.'

'That's all right Spills. I weren't lookin' for 'em,' Matt retorted.

Spills grimaced, swore thoughtfully. 'I got to get back to the ranch. Get this goddamn leg seen to.'

'Yeah, you do that,' Matt said and hauled away.

As he rode south, Matt went over the

past few days in his mind. None of what had happened mattered much to him, except Homer dying. After a while he climbed from the saddle, walked the grey a mile or so. Then he remounted, ran the horse towards where Tilly Welles would be.

18

Making of Plans

Grod Mitcham reached the Spills ranch at first dark. Finding the other hands had suppered and retired to the bunkhouse, he walked across the yard, knocked on the big, white-painted door of the main house.

Mitcham wanted to stall, needed time for Stockman and Rollo to get the cattle off Spills's land. He intended to spend most of the night jawing with his boss, while the herd got close to the sale pens outside Yuma. When there was no response to his knock, he turned the great latch ring and pushed open the door. He called Spills's name, then, slightly troubled at the quiet, he stepped back on to the terrace.

After thinking about it for a moment, he decided Spills had likely gone to town, but he was worried. The Spills ramrod sauntered back across the yard to the bunkhouse where some of the itinerant cowboys were playing blackjack.

'Anybody seen Mr Spills?'

The men shook their heads without looking up. But Frankie Chick, a long-time hand, raised his eyes.

'Maybe he's gone to town. What's up?' he asked.

'Seems there's a lot o' help missin'. Stockman, Rollo and Lemmer . . . one or two others that were workin' the bottom slopes. They should all've been back by now.'

Chick sniffed derisively. 'Happen they run across that 'breed, that hair-lifter we heard so much about. People round here get real skittish when his name's mentioned. 'Case', ain't it . . . his white man's name? Seems he goes on the warpath when he's put out any.'

'You don't know what you're talkin' about, Chick,' Mitcham snapped. 'Just get yourself ready for tomorrow. You'll likely be ridin' all day.' Angrily Mitcham left the bunkhouse. He was uncertain, knew something had gone wrong, and he saddled up a fresh horse.

As he rode, he was guessing, hoping that Spills had either gone to town or was paying the Welles girl another visit. Either way, when the loss of the cattle was finally discovered, he hoped to have the herd money safely stashed, be riding back with Stockman and Rollo.

For Coomer Spills, Mitcham had his story all worked out. He'd tell how they'd trailed cattle-thieves into the barren land and got ambushed in the gully, lost three men as well as the herd. Maybe then, by using a crooked truth, he'd get some back-up to take out the stumbling-block called Matt Case. Perhaps he'd call in on the Welles girl himself, offer his deceitful commiserations, console her after having sold out to Spills.

He single-footed his horse west, into the night. There was no real hurry. He didn't care about catching up with Stockman and the others, maybe having to swallow trail dust from the barrens.

★　★　★

When he emerged from the timbered slopes, Mitcham almost crossed Coomer Spills's way. He'd been escaping the full blast of the sun when he sighted the lone rider coming back from the direction of the gully.

At first he thought it was Stockman or one of the other hands riding back to meet up with him. But he drew back into the trees, saw it was Spills who rode past.

Mitcham cursed. He could see Spills was slumped forward, gripping the saddle horn. Then he saw the dark blood, thickly congealed across and down the man's leg. Spills's face was haggard, but determined and his eyes were set straight ahead.

It took Mitcham unawares, and it unnerved him. His mind raced, but he

209

sat the saddle very still. He watched the rancher until he was a long way past, half-expecting him to fall heavily from his horse.

The old man was nearly a mile off before Mitcham decided to make a move. He kicked his own horse, spurred it fast across the open country. He was headed for the high ground that fell sharply down behind the Spills ranch house.

It was a good hour before he slipped from his horse, hitched it in the shade at the back of the spread. He walked cautiously around the outbuildings, then waited until he saw Spills making his way across the yard that fronted the big house.

Three men came running from assorted worksheds. They ran to Spills and helped him down from his horse, carried him towards the house and up the steps while Mitcham slunk quietly around to the back porch.

With his gun in his hand, Mitcham stood with his back hard-pressed against the rear wall of the house. He was breathing deeply and his heart thumped with the fear of what might have happened, the aftermath of Spills's misadventure.

From inside the house, he heard an excited voice.

'You goin' to tell us what happened, boss?' the old ranch hand, Frankie Chick was asking. 'You want me to send someone into town for the doc?'

'No, you see to it, Frankie. It looks bad, but it ain't more'n a flesh wound. It's Mitcham I want. Where is he?' he asked savagely.

'He was here, askin' that o' *you*, boss. Not more'n a few hours ago.'

Mitcham gripped the butt of his gun until his hand shook. It was obvious that Spills had caught up with the stolen herd, that's where he'd got his wounds from. And he must have spoken at some time with one of his riders if not Stockman or Rollo. But now Mitcham didn't know what state the herd was in, whether it had been pushed on to the Yuma cattle pens or not. Then he recalled that he'd only hired Brendan Lemmer and two other men to drive cattle. They weren't in on the deal. It sounded like a mess, and knowing he had to stay and find out more, he cursed his luck.

'Case came through here. I think he was lookin' for Mitcham,' he heard Spills shout angrily. 'Told me about a herd bein' pushed Yuma way. So together, we went down to have a look for ourselves. We found Stockman and Clem Rollo all right. They had three new hands with 'em . . . drivin' my cattle through Copa Gully. Case and me, we just rode into the point, shot 'em dead.'

Mitcham heard the startled voices of disbelief. He cursed and hissed for them to keep quiet, waited for the silence to settle again.

'And that ain't the best part of it,' Spills went on. 'One o' them others . . . Lemmer. He spoke to me of my foreman. Said it was *his* plan they were hired to work to.'

'What you want us to do, boss?' Chick asked, supportively.

'Get out an' help bring back them beeves. But not you, Frankie. You got to help patch me up. Tie me to my saddle if you have to.'

'You goin' after Mitcham, boss?'

'Yeah, more'n that, when I've figured out where he's gone.'

Mitcham felt the cold shiver between his shoulder blades. He was about to back off when he heard Chick ask:

'What about him off the reservation . . . Matt Case? Who's he ridin' with then, boss?'

'Well, he ain't with us. But then again, he ain't against us. You men steer clear of him, though, you hear? I'll handle him when the time comes.'

Mitcham didn't wait to hear any more. He fast-tracked back to his horse and heeled away up the slope. He had frustration and anger burning through him now. His scheme was in ruins, and mostly due to the intervention of the 'breed called Matt Case. He checked the cylinder of his Colt and put his horse into a determined run, headed for Welles country.

19

The Expected Trail

Tilly heard the alarmed honking of the geese, rose startled from where she'd been sitting half-asleep on the porch. She looked out at the yard and home pasture for sign of a horse, but saw none, realized the sounds were from the back of the house. Perturbed, she reached out her hand to the front door, but it suddenly opened away from her, caught her off-balance.

'Mr Case? Matt?' she called. But the words died in her throat when she saw Grod Mitcham standing in the shadows of her main room.

The man's face was pouring with sweat, still blotched and ugly from his encounter with Matt. Tilly couldn't help thinking of a giant slice of pan-fried chicken and she withered, drew back in silent horror.

Mitcham stepped quickly forward and grabbed her wrist.

'No, it ain't him,' he sneered. 'So ain't that just too bad? Or possibly not, eh, pretty miss?'

'Get off me!' Tilly shouted, but Mitcham pulled her close. She smelled his hot, muggy odour and clawed her fingers at his face. He cursed and dragged her back into the house. Tilly lashed out with her feet, but Mitcham's strength was too much and he hurled her down on to the couch.

'You little wolverine,' he said, holding his fingers to the side of his face.

'I've done you no harm,' she cried. 'Leave me alone. Get out of my house.'

'Shut your mouth,' Mitcham told her. 'You make another sound like that an' I'll mark you. I'll cut you so's your *metis* friend won't recognize you when he gets here.'

All colour drained from Tilly's face and she started to tremble uncontrollably. All she wanted now was for Matt

Case to return. She tried to reconcile herself to virtue in hostility, in Matt Case, and immediately hated herself for doing it.

Mitcham wiped blood across his face, on to his chin. 'Seems you get yourself a front-row seat when me an' him meet,' he snarled. 'Only this time the endin's goin' to be different, eh, missy?'

Tilly felt impulsive despair. She leaped to her feet and raced for the door across the room. But Mitcham had seen it coming and was too quick. He placed himself in the doorway and as she lunged at him he gave a dead-bone grin.

'Yeah, that's it missy,' he said. 'A man like me can take that an' more.'

Tilly lashed out with her foot and caught him low in the leg. Mitcham threw a punch at her head and she felt the hard, dark thud. Then she felt herself being grabbed, lifted bodily from the floor. There was a wild rush of air, then a smack of pain across her

217

body, Mitcham walked over to where he'd thrown her. He grabbed her by the hair and pulled her to her feet. He ripped the top of her blouse from her shoulders while Tilly ripped at the hang of his bottom lip. She tore it open and Mitcham smashed her down to the floor again.

Tilly tried to rise, to stay awake and warn Matt. But her hands slid away from her and she collapsed with her cheek against the floorboards she'd so recently scrubbed. She sobbed just once at the terrible irony, then lost her senses as the painful dark enveloped her.

20

Mixed Blood

It was mid-afternoon when Matt Case rode into the yard of the Welles ranch. The whole place was quiet, and from the moment he'd started down the grassy slope he'd felt an uneasy tension gripping his vitals. The geese were nipping at long grass in the orchard and there was no sign of Tilly.

He watched the house closely, half-expecting her to come out and greet him, curious to know what had happened. As he rode towards the house, he rehearsed just how he'd tell her that the trouble with her neighbour, Coomer Spills, was no more.

He reined in at the hitch rail, remained saddled to lash out with his boot as the geese came running, swore he'd kill them if Mitcham didn't get him first. Then he rolled stiffly from his horse, dropped the reins as he saw movement from behind the front window. He slapped the grey's rump, had only taken one step when the window shutter was smashed open and a gun roared at him.

Matt felt the warm pulse of air as the bullet closely missed his left eye. He dropped to a crouch but held his fire, uncertain about Tilly's whereabouts.

The gun roared again, but this time the bullet broke into his left shoulder, sent him twisting to the ground. 'Mitcham,' he said as he rolled with the impact. Another bullet came, gouting the hard-packed yard dirt into his face. He continued to roll, seeking shelter below the low, planked veranda of the house. Each turn sent pain stabbing deep into his chest, up into his neck.

When he got to the relative safety of the corner of the house he got to his feet. His left arm was already unusable, his left hand rigid with pain. He grabbed his Colt with his right hand before he dropped it, worked his way down the side of the house to the water trough. He looked at his reflection in the water, wanted to take a breather. Then he heard the clump of boot steps from inside, just as another bullet tore through the small side window. He grinned, mumbled, 'stupid, he's goin' to kill you,' and doubled over.

He went on and turned across the rear of the house. He banged on the scullery door, ran faster right the way around the building, until he came to the front corner. He took six quiet steps to the front door and stopped for a moment. Then he pushed his Colt back into his waistband, called on his forebears for strength and lifted the latch.

As he hoped, Mitcham was coming through the house, from the back, where he'd heard Matt bang on the scullery door. He fired on instinct, but Matt leaped to the side, threw himself to the floor as he came in. Through the instant tear of pain, he saw Tilly. She was looking at him, raising herself from behind the couch. He held out his right hand, hoped she'd stay down.

But she was still dazed, looked at him through scared, confused eyes. Matt realized then what had happened, and a grimace bent the features of his face.

He stepped up and faced Mitcham, gulped when he saw the bloody mess of the man's face. He stood still, daring Mitcham to fire because he'd been counting. But the closeness of certain death for one of them was too much for Mitcham and another bullet buried itself in the wall planks behind him.

'Stay down!' Matt yelled at Tilly while staring into Mitcham's eyes. He'd got it right, though; Mitcham had fired his last bullet and had to reload.

Matt felt like apologizing, for using the advantage of thinking. But instead, he drew the Colt from his waistband with his right hand and with a cheerless shake of his head, he steadied himself and fired. The first shot ripped low into Mitcham's neck, the second and third into his chest and belly. The flagging ramrod's feet did a shuffle forward, then he staggered back, his legs buckled and he went down.

Mitcham was a big man and had a few moments of life left in him. He cursed and held his shattered neck with one hand, swung his gun up with the other. The empty chambers made their dull, empty clicks as the ceiling above him began its final swirl. He dropped the gun, and raised his arm, twisted his fingers into the fabric of Tilly's newly tacked-up curtains.

Tilly looked at the still-smoking gun in Matt's hand and collapsed to the floor again. But Matt was there fast and helped to break her fall. With one arm he clumsily helped her to her feet, noticed the dark bruise high on the side of her face as he walked her to the couch.

'Don't get up 'til I come back,' he said sternly.

Matt went over to Mitcham, saw the slight flicker of an eyelid. He bent low for the man's last words.

'Why'd you get involved in this?' Mitcham burbled through the foaming blood that filled his mouth. 'A man like you . . . ' But the man was dead before he finished the sentence.

'I only went to help an old man. The rest was down to you,' Matt responded bitterly.

He pushed the Colt back into his waistband and pulled off his coat, then blinked at the pain when he saw his bloodied arm and shoulder. He turned away from Tilly, roughly twisted his shirtsleeve tight around the wound. The searing pain made him curse long and loud as he dragged the heavy body across the yard. But he didn't stop until he'd made the ground between the fruit trees. He let go his grip of Mitcham's sweat-stained collar, watched the man's meaty face bite deep into the grass.

'Eat goddamn worms, you son-of-a-bitch, white man,' he said coldly.

★ ★ ★

Back in the house, the cloying heat and cordite fumes almost overcame him. He looked at his shoulder and his arm, ground his teeth with the pain. But now Tilly saw the blood running to his fingers, was already on her feet.

'Outside on the rocker,' she said curtly. 'Now I'm taking control.'

Twenty minutes later, after finishing the last of his forty-rod, Matt closed his eyes as Tilly administered warm water, salve and a bandage.

'The bullet might still be in there,' she was saying. 'We'll have to get you into town, first thing. Doc Pease needs to see these wounds.'

But Matt's mind was elsewhere.

'I had a little animal once . . . never knew what it was. I kept it in a box,' he said ruefully. 'When it died, I poked it down a hole in the riverbank. Seems the least I could do for Mitcham.'

'With one hand, you poked him down a hole?' Tilly asked in disbelief.

'No. I thought about it though. When Coomer Spills gets here, as he surely will, he's goin' to feel real cheated when he finds Mitcham's body. So I'll leave the buryin' to him. A gesture o' my good will.'

'Well, I'm glad I won't be here to see it,' Tilly said.

'You're goin? Leavin' the ranch? But I thought — '

'Then you thought wrong . . . like me,' she interjected. 'I loathe just about everything there is in White Basin. Mr Spills is welcome to *all* of it.'

Matt had himself a few moments of thought before he spoke.

'I've had a look around, like my pa told me, an' he was right. But he only spoke about the richness of the land, not about those who own it.' Matt relaxed a little as the salve began its work. 'In the way down here from the north, I rode through Montana . . . along the Yellowstone,' he said. 'There's a lot o' free country, Tilly, an' not much in the way o' killin'. So perhaps now I'll try there. It looked like somewhere my ma would have spoke well of.'

Tilly looked Matt in the eye. 'Sounds almost too good to be true. Perhaps I'll leave Mr Spills a forwarding address for somewhere along the Yellowstone, shall I?' she asked.

Matt opened one eye, nodded diffidently. 'You'd be real good company ma'am . . . real good,' he said quietly.

'Well that *is* good, then.' Tilly declared with a smile. 'But right now, perhaps you'd like to stay for something to eat. I can't ask you what you'd really like, though. There's not that much.'

While he thought of an answer, Matt untied his beaded waistband. With one hand, he wrapped it around his Colt, tossed the bundle across the veranda.

'There's enough,' he said, with a slow, wicked grin. 'I got me a hankerin' for a big mess o' goose. Roast goose, with apple trimmin's.'

We do hope that you have enjoyed reading this large print book.

Did you know that all of our titles are available for purchase?

We publish a wide range of high quality large print books including:
Romances, Mysteries, Classics
General Fiction
Non Fiction and Westerns

Special interest titles available in large print are:
The Little Oxford Dictionary
Music Book, Song Book
Hymn Book, Service Book

Also available from us courtesy of Oxford University Press:
Young Readers' Dictionary
(large print edition)
Young Readers' Thesaurus
(large print edition)

For further information or a free brochure, please contact us at:
Ulverscroft Large Print Books Ltd.,
The Green, Bradgate Road, Anstey,
Leicester, LE7 7FU, England.
Tel: (00 44) **0116 236 4325**
Fax: (00 44) **0116 234 0205**

Other titles in the
Linford Western Library:

A TOWN CALLED TROUBLESOME

John Dyson

Matt Matthews had carved his ranch out of the wild Wyoming frontier. But he had his troubles. The big blow of '86 was catastrophic, with dead beeves littering the plains, and the oncoming winter presaged worse. On top of this, a gang of desperadoes had moved into the Snake River valley, killing, raping and rustling. All Matt can do is to take on the killers single-handed. But will he escape the hail of lead?

THE WIND WAGON

Troy Howard

Sheriff Al Corning was as tough as they came and with his four seasoned deputies he kept the peace in Laramie — at least until the squatters came. To fend off starvation, the settlers took some cattle off the cowmen, including Jonas Lefler. A hard, unforgiving man, Lefler retaliated with lynchings. Things got worse when one of the squatters revealed he was a former Texas lawman — and no mean shooter. Could Sheriff Corning prevent further bloodshed?

CABEL

Paul K. McAfee

Josh Cabel returned home from the
Civil War to find his family all
murdered by rioting members of
Quantrill's band. The hunt for the
killers led Josh to Colorado City
where, after months of searching, he
finally settled down to work on a
ranch nearby. He saved the life of an
Indian, who led him to a cache of
weapons waiting for Sitting Bull's
attack on the Whites. His involvement threw Cabel into grave danger.
When the final confrontation came,
who had the fastest — and deadlier
— draw?

RIVERBOAT

Alan C. Porter

When Rufus Blake died he was found to be carrying a gold bar from a Confederate gold shipment that had disappeared twenty years before. This inspires Wes Hardiman and Ben Travis to swap horse and trail for a riverboat, the *River Queen*, on the Mississippi, in an effort to find the missing gold. Cord Duval is set on destroying the *River Queen* and he has the power and the gunmen to do it. Guns blaze as Hardiman and Travis attempt to unravel the mystery and stay alive.

MCKINNEY'S LAW

Mike Stotter

McKinney didn't count on coming across a dead body in the middle of Texas. He was about to become involved in an ever-deepening mystery. The renegade Comanche warrior, Black Eagle, was on the loose, creating havoc; he didn't appear in McKinney's plans at all, not until the Comanche forced himself into his life. The US Army gave McKinney some relief to his problems, but it also added to them, and with two old friends McKinney set about bringing justice through his own law.

BLACK RIVER

Adam Wright

John Dyer has come to the insignificant little town of Black River to destroy the last living reminder of his dark past. He has come to kill. Jack Hart is determined to stop him. Only he knows the terrible truth that has driven Dyer here, and he knows that only he can beat Dyer in a gunfight. Ex-lawman Brad Harris is after Dyer too — to avenge his family. The stage is set for madness, death and vengeance.